THE PATROLMAN GOT OUT
AND CAME TOWARD HER.

"My friend Roy!" Stella cried. "At the Sierra Motel — we have drinks, me and Roy. He talk funny, crazy. I think maybe he will hurt himself!"

"Okay, miss, go on, we'll follow you."

When they reached the Sierra again, Stella led the police to unit fifteen. The door was locked. One policeman went for the manager. The other pounded the door. There was no response.

When the policeman returned with the manager and the keys, they went inside. Stella Ortega screamed.

The body hung from the center beam . . . .

HERE'S WHAT THE CRITICS SAID:

"Crowe keeps all this moving with a taut line that marks a real pro." *The New York Times*

"This is just the first in a series of hits." *Kirkus Reviews*

"This is the first of a projected series about violence in America today, and if all are as good as this one, Crowe can sit side by side with his peers." Hartford, Conn. *Courant*

"The scene moves from a ranch to a mental hospital, assorted slum areas and countryside. Fast-paced and mystifying." Columbus, Ohio *Dispatch*

"As everybody knows, sins make for good reading— at least in mystery novels." St. Louis, Mo. *Post-Dispatch*

"This is the provocative first of a projected new series." *Publishers Weekly*

"Pattern of flight and pursuit good. Mr. Crowe's new county is an attractive setting." San Francisco *Examiner Chronicle*

Another way to die

John Crowe

MANOR
BOOKS
INC.

To Ben and Marian,
for hard work and good times

A MANOR BOOK 1973

Manor Books Inc.
329 Fifth Avenue
New York, New York 10016

Library of Congress Catalog Card Number: 77-37034

Another way to die

Highways — — — — — — — — — — Towns •

1

Two barren mountain chains fill most of Buena Costa County—the main Coast Range that reaches from the great San Joaquin Valley inland, and the Santa Ysolde Mountains that touch the sea. Steep, rough, dry semi-desert, the canyons belong to wild pigs, coyotes, bears, snakes, the last cougars. Between the ranges are narrow ranching valleys, and the Monteverde Plateau in the north. These small valleys, and the mountains, form ninety-eight percent of the county.

The remaining two percent is where the people live —the long, narrow strip of mild coastal slope like the Garden of Eden at the edge of the blue sea. The beautiful coast, rich and brilliant with palms and hibiscus, where travelers come from across the world to the lush, lazy old capital city of San Vicente like some jewel of the Mediterranean.

One traveler, a soldier, came walking along Dune Drive on the outskirts of San Vicente at 5:10 P.M. that Monday. The evening was warm and clear for Buena Costa County in May, and the day man at the Sierra Motel saw the soldier a long way off. The day man watched the soldier grow from a speck into a blond young man who carried a canvas suitcase and looked straight ahead. The soldier turned into the Sierra Motel.

The soldier's boots and uniform were dusty and his tie hung loose in the warm evening. There were sergeant's stripes on his arms, and three rows of medal ribbons on his chest.

"A room," the soldier said. "Unit fifteen if it's empty."

The day man hesitated. It was unusual for guests to arrive on foot. But business was slow, the soldier had a suitcase, and he knew unit fifteen so couldn't be a total stranger. Unit fifteen was the best the Sierra had to offer— farthest from the road and closest to the beach.

"Okay," the day man said. "You from around here?"

"Yes," the soldier said. He signed the register: Roy Scott, U.S. Army, Vietnam.

"No stateside address?" the day man said.

"No," Roy Scott said. "Where can I buy a record player?"

"This late? King Discount out by the university, maybe."

"Call me a taxi. Half an hour."

"Sure thing, Sergeant," the day man said.

The soldier, Roy Scott, took his dusty suitcase to unit fifteen. The day man called the taxi. When it arrived, the soldier came out shaved and clean.

*

Mr. James Byers, manager of the Sierra, took over the desk at 6:30 P.M. Loud music was coming from unit fifteen.

"What the hell's that?" Byers asked the day man.

"The music? I don't know. Classical stuff."

"I mean who's playing it? Is it a radio?"

"Record player, I guess." The day man told Byers about the soldier.

"Roy Scott?" Byers said. "One of Ben Scott's boys was in the army, I think. The rancher owns half the valley."

"He didn't give any local address," the day man said.

"No," Byers said. "I guess it couldn't be."

The music—elegant and vigorous—went on after the day man left. After a time, the manager realized that it was the same record playing over and over—some classical dance tune. Byers called unit fifteen and told the soldier to tone it down. The volume went low at once. Byers liked that, the soldier wasn't a troublemaker.

At 8:30 another taxi appeared. The music from unit fifteen stopped, and the soldier went off in the taxi.

*

Byers was seated in front of the motel office at 10:30 P.M. when an old blue Ford drove up to unit fifteen. The young sergeant got out with a man and a woman. The newcomers were both in their late thirties and had the dark faces of Mexicans. Byers didn't like Mexicans at the motel, but the way it was these days, even in Buena Costa County, he was reluctant to do anything without a solid excuse.

5

At 11:00 P.M. Byers took a walk around the grounds. Above the sound of the surf he heard voices and the clink of ice in glasses in unit fifteen. That was all, and Byers went back to his chair outside the office. At 11:30 they all came out of unit fifteen, and drove away in the blue Ford.

Neither the Ford nor the soldier returned by 1:00 A.M. when Byers turned off all the motel lights except the one at the office and lay down on a cot in the room behind the office.

Sometime after 2:00 A.M. Byers heard a car drive up, but no one came into the office, so he went to sleep.

*

The music filtered slowly into Byers' mind, barely audible. It was the same record, playing over and over again. Byers looked at his watch: 3:10 A.M. He lay awake, expecting his telephone to start ringing with the complaints of other guests. But no one called, and Byers tried to fall back to sleep.

He couldn't. Each time the low music stopped, he lay as if there were a weight on him. He held his breath, sure that this time it wouldn't start again. Then it did start, as maddening as the drip of a faucet.

Byers got up, went to the telephone. He could hear the ringing off in unit fifteen. The voice that finally answered was low and tense, with a question in it, as if the man had been staring at the phone before picking it up.

"Who's out there? Hello? Is someone out there?"

Byers said, "Sergeant Scott? This is the manager. You know what the hell time it is?"

A silence, and then, "Time? Where?"

"It's three-thirty A.M.! Turn that music off."

Another silence, as if the soldier's brain worked slowly, and the slow voice said, "You don't like the music? Very noble music. A dance. Don't you want to dance, Mr. Manager?"

"Turn it off now, Sergeant. You understand me?"

"Yes. I understand you."

The soldier hung up. Byers went to a window. He saw a small car, a Mustang, parked in front of unit fifteen. Maybe the damned soldier was a troublemaker after all. The music stopped. Byers waited ten minutes at the window. The record didn't begin again. Byers went back to his cot.

*

In unit fifteen, Stella Ortega sat on the bed with her knees drawn up under a long man's robe. She held a glass of whiskey, her thin young face drawn like unhealthy parchment over its delicate bones. Her black eyes were nervous.

"Maybe I should oughta go, Roy," she said.

Roy Scott went to the small record player. He was bare to the waist and barefooted. He turned the machine off, watched the record slow to a stop.

"It's not you, Stell. The music. You like the music?"

"I don' know that kind of music," Stella said. "I don' listen much to no music."

"It's been hard for you, Stell?"

Stella Ortega shrugged her thin shoulders. "Who I blame? I got no kick 'cept against myself, Roy."

"Did anyone try to make it better for you? Anyone care what you needed, wanted? Everyone wants, everyone grabs, no one helps."

Stella Ortega drank. "Why'd you find me, Roy?"

"You're a friend, Stell. You're a pretty girl."

"I ain't so pretty no more. You need a friend, need a girl, so bad you got to look for me?"

"I guess so," Roy Scott said. "You, maybe Helen and Pelé, my father, a couple more."

"Three years you don' see us."

"Maybe I needed some real people now."

He stood at the record player and patted at his bare chest as if looking for pockets in his flesh. He went to where his uniform jacket hung over a chair, took a small, thin cigarette from the breast pocket. He offered another to Stella Ortega. She shook her head. As he lighted his, he stared down at his jacket with its sergeant's stripes and rows of ribbons. He drew the acrid marijuana smoke deep into his lungs, held it, and let it out slowly. He looked toward the record player.

"They want me to dance," he said. "I won't dance."

Out in the night a mockingbird ran through its songs.

"Noble music," Roy said. "Did you listen, Stell? Noble and elegant. Something to dance for. Not now."

Stella said, "I don' know what you talk about, Roy."

"A dead dance, Stell. A noble dance turned slimy. They call it life, and it's no good. Not the way the music plays now. Not noble, no. It never was, but there was the illusion, and they could believe then."

He sat down. Stella left the bed, sat on the arm of his chair, began to stroke his bare chest.

"I remember, Stell, but what's real? What's illusion?"

Stella said, "Maybe you sleep now, Roy?"

"Do you sleep, Stell?"

"Sometimes I sleep real good, you know?"

"That's one way, I guess. The happy dust," Roy Scott said, and touched her. "Go home, Stell. Sleep good. Go on now."

Stella watched him, puzzled. "Roy? Is it okay?"

"Sure, Stell, it's all fine. Be good, okay?"

He watched her while she dressed. He was smiling, drawing the marijuana deep, enjoying it. Stella dressed quickly. She kissed him when she left.

Outside in her old Mustang, she heard the music start. As low as it could be turned. Her hands shook as she listened. The elegant dance stopped—and started again. A chair was moved inside the unit, then creaked as if stood on. The record stopped. Stella put her shaking hand on the car door to get out.

The record began again. Stella bit her lip, and sat for a time, her hands shaking violently now. The music went on.

Stella started the Mustang.

*

Half awake, Byers heard the car drive away. A small car, probably the Mustang at unit fifteen. Muttering, Byers rolled over and tried to get back to sleep. He would tell the damned soldier to leave first thing tomorrow.

*

Stella Ortega parked at a frame house in the slums of San Vicente. Nothing moved in the city in the silent dark past 4:00 A.M. Stella knocked a signal on the door of the frame house. The door opened, and she went inside.

Byers heard the Mustang return only a few minutes after it had gone. Damn! Or was it the Mustang? Time moved in and out of sleep for Byers. Time and space. Some car drove somewhere. A few minutes or hours. Byers groaned.

Someone walked somewhere.

Byers slept. No one came near the office.

*

It was after 5:00 A.M. when Stella Ortega came out of the front door of the old frame house in the San Vicente slums. She walked calmly. Her hands were steady. She went to her car—and stopped in the dark night. She blinked on the street as if she had just remembered something. Her thin face became agitated again. She stood for a full minute. Then she got into the Mustang and drove off south—toward Dune Drive.

At the Sierra Motel she parked and ran to the door of unit fifteen. There was thin light inside behind drawn shades. There was no sound. Stella knocked.

"Roy? Roy, honey?"

She knocked harder. There was no answer. Stella ran back to her car, drove toward the city proper again. In the 800 block of Calle Real she saw the police car. She blew her horn, and stopped. A patrolman got out of the police car, came toward her.

"My friend Roy!" Stella cried. "At the Sierra Motel! I think he is bad! He—"

"That's the county, miss. We're city police. If you'll give me your name, we'll contact the sheriff's—"

"Stella Ortega. We have drinks, me and Roy. He talk funny, crazy. I think maybe he will hurt himself!"

"Okay, miss, go on, we'll follow you."

When they reached the Sierra again, Stella led the police to unit fifteen. The door was locked. One policeman went for the manager. The other pounded on the door. There was no response.

Manager Byers arrived with the keys. He cursed the damned soldier. The policemen went inside. Byers and Stella Ortega followed them. Stella screamed.

The body hung from the center beam.

A sergeant's uniform lay on a chair. The record player was turning silently. Byers sat down. One policeman ran to call in. Stella Ortega stared up at the hanging man.

"But . . . that is not Roy," she said. "I don' know that man!"

2

"You don't know who the dead man is," Lee Beckett said, "or what happened to the soldier?"

"No on both," County Prosecutor Charles Tucker said. "And it's no suicide. The autopsy showed he died of a fractured skull. He was dead when he was strung up."

Lee Beckett looked out at San Vicente brilliant in the morning sun below his living-room window. A heavy-shouldered man of fifty-two, as thick as he was wide, he seemed shorter than his six feet. His gray hair was cropped short and his blue eyes were sunk in wind creases.

"Tell me the details, Charley," he said.

Charles Tucker was a thin man with a young face, three inches taller than Beckett and fifteen years younger. At thirty-seven, he was a bright young man on the way up. His voice was firm and brisk.

"Dead man's a Caucasian, between thirty and thirty-five, medium height, blond hair. The rope was clothesline. An overturned chair under the body. No clothes in the unit except Roy Scott's uniform. No money, personal effects, or identification anywhere, not even in the uniform, except a sales slip from King Discount for a record player charged on a BankAmericard in the name of Roy Scott. A bottle of Scotch, four used glasses, an empty pill bottle, two marijuana cigarettes, and an empty canvas suitcase. The record player was still turning, record on the last groove."

"No unclaimed car?" Beckett said.

"No car. If the victim came in a car, Roy Scott, or someone, took it. Scott walked into the motel."

"Time?"

"The victim died between three-thirty A.M. and five-thirty. The S.V.P.D. men arrived at five-thirty. The guy'd been hit more than once, his nose was broken, too."

"That Ortega girl was there until four A.M.?"

"She couldn't have killed him, Lee. She weighs a hundred and two, thin as a straw. The victim weighs at least a hundred and fifty, and he was hit awful hard with something."

"She could have had help. Sheriff Hoag holding her?"

"For now," Tucker said. "She's sticking by her story. It could be true, but she's a B-girl with four years of arrests, and there's an hour missing from her story. I think she was getting a shot of heroin. Her arm's full of holes."

Tucker watched Beckett as he said the last. He saw the big man stiffen. Beckett turned from the window.

"Is that why you want to appoint me special investigator for you, Charley? I'll hound any junkie to the grave?"

"I didn't say that, Lee."

"No, you didn't say it." Beckett went back to the window.

Charles Tucker said, "All right, drugs could be the key. That was your beat the two years in the sheriff's office."

"Three years ago," Beckett said. "Old history."

"Roy Scott met two other people last night, Lee. Older. Mexican-Americans like the Ortega girl. You could know them."

"What else, Charley?"

"Your experience, Lee. Who hangs a dead man? A psycho? Maybe we'll need all the experience we can get."

"Nuts!" Beckett turned. "Why a special investigator at all? It's Sheriff Hoag's work. Why is he turning it over to you? It's not like Hoag to turn over any case."

Charles Tucker sat down on a couch. Beckett watched him. The prosecutor spoke like a man choosing his words.

"Roy Scott is the oldest son of Ben Scott, Lee. Ben is the biggest rancher in the Santa Ysolde Valley. He's on the boards of three banks, owns half the county. Hoag's up for re-election this year, you know that, and Ben Scott's his major backer. Hoag sees only bad in this for him. If he clears Roy Scott, they'll say he was easy on the boy. If he gets Roy convicted, maybe killed, they'll say he worked too hard to prove his honesty, and maybe he loses Ben Scott. I'm not up for re-election this time. But you know my staff—three kids with no real experience because I've got no budget. Hoag wants to turn it over to me, rule himself out because of his relation to the Scotts, but he doesn't want anyone saying the case didn't get the best police work. He thinks you're the answer—the best detective around, with no angles or ax to grind."

"You don't have to take it, Charley," Beckett said. "I think Hoag's right, he is too close to the Scotts."

"And it couldn't hurt your office to solve it."

Tucker studied his hands. "It couldn't hurt."

"You'll make governor yet, Charley."

"I need your help, Lee."

Beckett looked out at the greenhouses of his nursery. He had been in Buena Costa County for six years, owned the nursery for three, but he had been a detective for twenty-five years before that, here and in New York.

"Okay, Charley," Beckett said, and sat down. "Now, where did that rope come from and what was in that pill bottle?"

"Roy Scott bought the rope at King Discount yesterday. The bottle had been used for Benzedrine pills."

Beckett rested his head on the back of his chair. "He gave his address as Vietnam, bought a rope, was in a motel less than twenty miles from his home, played one record over and over, told the Ortega girl 'I won't dance,' acted unstable. All the sounds of a suicidal psycho. Only something happened to change it to murder, unless it was all an act. Something between four A.M. and five-thirty, if the Ortega girl is telling the truth, but you can't trust any addict."

"The motel manager says everything seemed okay up until four A.M."

"So we'll say that the dead man did show up sometime after four. He was killed by blows on the head, then strung up. Maybe in some attempt to make us think it was suicide, at least for a time, maybe for some other reason.

Whatever, it looks like the soldier ran in the victim's clothes, probably because he knew a uniform would be easy to spot. He could have taken all identification by accident, or it could have been another attempt to fool the police. How much does the dead man look like this Roy Scott?"

"Just in general appearance," Tucker said. "Roy is twenty-five, the same medium height, and also a blond. They're not enough alike to fool anyone who knew Roy Scott."

"But it was pure chance that the Ortega girl came back with the police so soon—if her story's true. Roy Scott could have hoped the victim would be taken for him for a time. The time to get away after switching suicide to murder."

Tucker said, "Unless Roy didn't kill him. Roy could be another victim, even kidnapped. Ben Scott is rich."

"Anything is possible," Beckett agreed. "You go to work on the dead man, find out who he was. And, Charley, I work my own way, yes? You don't pull a Hoag on me?"

Tucker nodded. "I've got your credentials, a pic of Roy Scott, and Hoag's report on the case so far."

"Put them on the table, Charley," Beckett said.

When the prosecutor had gone, Beckett sat for a time without moving. Twenty-three years a New York city cop—from rookie to detective captain. Until an addict's bomb blew his home and his life apart. One son dead; himself in the hospital for six months; his wife crippled, in a wheelchair. So he brought her West to a new life that lasted one year before she died, and took a job in the sheriff's office to forget. To forget, and to hound all drug users and sellers to hell and beyond.

Two more years a detective before John Hoag became sheriff. There was no way Beckett could work with a sheriff like John Hoag. He quit, started his nursery, enjoyed his nursery. But there were still criminals, addicts, psychos. To be hunted. And Beckett had never really quit.

*

In the May morning sun, Sheriff John Hoag parked his official car in the driveway of the Charro Ranch. A stocky man of fifty, Hoag had a smooth, bland face that revealed nothing, offended no one. As he got out of his car now in front of the low, sprawling ranch house, he stood for a moment looking at the silent house. Then he walked around the house toward the sound of men and horses in a nearby corral.

A stocky, muscular youth in denim work clothes and riding boots, his dark hair worn long, prepared to saddle a young, quivering horse held roped by three cowhands in the center of the corral. At the fence, a short, broad older man, with a thick mustache and close-set pale eyes shaded by a wide-brimmed straw Stetson, called sharp orders to the men holding the horse.

Hoag walked up to the broad man at the fence. "Ham ride as good as his brother, Rhine?" the sheriff said, leaning on the fence to watch the youthful rider.

"Better," the older man said, his sun-wrinkled eyes approving the young man out in the corral. "Roy rides okay, but he's no athlete, Sheriff, no rancher like Ham."

"Guess not. Fast cars, not fast horses for Roy, eh, Jess?" Hoag said. "He around now? Roy, I mean?"

"Ain't seen him," Jess Rhine said, and watched the youth in the corral, Ham Scott, mount the quivering horse.

"Know where I might find Roy?" Hoag said.

"No, I ain't seen Roy for—" The broad man, Jess Rhine, stopped and looked at the sheriff. "You looking for Roy for something, Sheriff? More trouble?"

"Has Roy gone somewhere, Jess?"

"I'm ranch foreman, Hoag. Roy works in town. I got no reason to know where Roy is or ain't. Don't suck around me with your tricks! You want to talk about Roy, you go talk to Ben Scott!"

"No trick, Jess," Hoag said mildly. "I thought maybe your girl might have talked about Roy to you."

"Janice is Ham's girl. Why would she talk about Roy?"

"Maybe I better talk to Ham, then," Hoag said.

"Maybe you better talk to Ben," Jess Rhine snapped. "He likes people to use the front door, especially his friends."

Sheriff Hoag's smooth face showed no reaction. He leaned on the fence for a few more seconds, watched Ham Scott hanging onto the bucking horse out in the corral, and then turned and walked back around the ranch house to the front door. A Japanese houseman answered his ring, and ushered him into a vast living room with rough white adobe walls, heavy brown ceiling beams, and French doors at the far end that opened onto a large brick patio and a blue swimming pool. Two people were in the room—a man who stood with his back to the patio, and a woman who sat on a couch.

"Hello, John," the man said, "what brings you so early?"

"I'm looking for Roy, Ben," Hoag said.

Ben Scott said, "Roy? Why?"

He was a small man with a soft, round face like some aged schoolboy. An indoor face, unweathered by sun or wind, and his small body had gone heavy with the years. He was fifty-five, despite the schoolboy look and dark hair without a trace of gray. There was quick authority in his manner and movements, and his sharp eyes were alert behind horn-rimmed glasses. He wore gray slacks, white shirt and tie, and an incongruous old brown corduroy jacket and high-heeled western boots. His eyes were suddenly worried, alarmed.

"Why do you want Roy, John?" he said again.

Hoag said, "Have you seen him in the last two days?"

"No, we haven't," Ben Scott said, and looked at the woman.

"No, John," Marlene Scott said.

She sat on a modern couch of pale wood and red tweed. All the furniture in the room was ultra-modern, clashing with the adobe walls and red-tiled floor—chrome-and-steel, leather-and-glass, pale wood and bright fabric shaped in body contours. A free-standing fireplace in the center of the room was in violent war with the old brick fireplace that filled the left wall, unused and partly screened off.

"You better sit down, John, and tell us," Marlene Scott said. Her voice was low and firm, but there was a hesitation in it now.

Sheriff Hoag sat down. He told them. Ben Scott listened, his round face going slack, his eyes clouding. Marlene Scott studied the floor. She was a small, trim woman of maybe forty-two, curved at breasts and hips, but not soft. Her fine face was all soft hollows and sharp bones, a skin like polished china, each shiny strand of her blond hair in place. She matched with the sleek, modern furniture, not with the rustic adobe-and-oak room. When Hoag finished, she said nothing for a time, smoothed her skirt.

Ben Scott said, "Roy was in San Vicente last night? At some motel? He didn't even call us!"

"What about the way he was acting, Ben?" Sheriff Hoag said. "Half crazy, that record, the rope?"

"How do I know how he was acting? Who saw him? How do we know it really was Roy? He—"

Hoag said, "It was Roy, Ben. His pic was identified."

Marlene Scott looked up. "You think he killed that man in the motel, John?"

"I didn't say that," Hoag said. "We don't know enough. All we know is that the man's dead, and Roy's missing."

"Missing?" Marlene said. "You mean that Roy could be dead somewhere, too, don't you, John?"

"Dead?" Ben Scott said, and the rancher sat down.

"There's no evidence of that, either," Hoag said.

The two Scotts said nothing. Each seemed to be alone with private visions. Ben Scott's soft face battled to hold together, keep control. His wife's face held too tight, as brittle as glass.

Sheriff Hoag crossed his legs. "Roy was supposed to stay here at the ranch with you two after that trouble last month, right?" he said.

"He went away a few—" Marlene Scott began.

"A few days ago," Ben Scott said. He stood up again, walked. "We don't know where he went or why, John, I'm sorry. I suppose we should have told you, that court order and all, but he seemed to be getting along so well. Doing a good, steady job of work for me in the office, just the way he'd been doing before that Ted Andrewski got to him."

Hoag nodded. "I understand, Ben."

"John?" Marlene Scott said. "Where is he now? He ran from that motel at five A.M. You're hunting him. Where is he, what is he doing?"

"I don't know, Marlene," Hoag said. He took a photograph from his pocket, handed it to Ben Scott. "That's the man who was killed. Know him, Ben?"

Ben Scott studied the photo. "No. I don't know him."

"Marlene?" Hoag said.

Marlene Scott looked at the picture. She looked at it for some time. It was a morgue photo. She shivered. "I never saw anyone like that, no."

Hoag took the photo. "I want you two to be honest, no heroics. Has anyone contacted you about Roy? Anyone ask you for money? Any kind of unusual call?"

"No," Ben Scott said. "You think Roy's been—?"

"You're a rich man, Ben," Hoag said. "If anyone does contact you, you'll tell me? Right away?"

"Yes, of course, damn it!" Ben Scott said, paced.

Sheriff Hoag stood up. "I've decided to turn the case officially over to Charles Tucker's office for now. That way there'll be no chance of a prejudice charge later. Tucker'll appoint a special investigator, Lee Beckett. He was a New York city detective captain. He's good and experienced."

The Scotts were silent. Marlene watched Sheriff Hoag, her face drawn tight over its classic bones. "You're a careful man, John," she said.

Hoag's face was bland, neutral. "I think it's best."

"Beckett?" Ben Scott said. "Damn it, isn't he extra tough, a little unbalanced? Something about his family?"

"He'll handle the investigation, but I'll keep a close eye on him," Hoag said. "You understand, Ben?"

Ben Scott nodded slowly. "All right, yes."

Hoag started for the door, stopped. "Was Roy working on anything special for you, Ben? I ought to know."

"No, nothing special. Just in my office."

"Good," Hoag said. "If Roy calls, let me know first, right? Not Tucker or Beckett. Call me."

They both nodded as Hoag left.

3

San Vicente has always been the heart of Buena Costa County, since the first Spaniard sailed into the harbor four hundred years ago, and the first Spaniard walked up from Mexico in his armor two hundred years later. Clinging to its green strip of coast, protected by the Santa Ysolde Mountains from the hot winds of the empty back country, its even climate is often misty when the sun is hot and bright twenty miles away in the Santa Ysolde Valley.

The May morning mist had just begun to lift when Lee Beckett walked into the office of the Sierra Motel. Both the day man and the manager, Byers, were there. Byers jumped when he saw Beckett.

"Mr. Beckett," the manager said. "I haven't seen you walking on our beach much any more."

"I walk," Beckett said. "I want you two to tell me about the trouble last night."

"You're back with the sheriff?" Byers said.

"Tucker's office. Talk about last night."

Byers told his story of the night, and the day man added what he had seen.

Beckett thought about it for a time. "The dead man couldn't have been one of the people who came back with Roy Scott the first time? The man?"

Byers shook his head. "They was both Mexican. The guy was bigger, too. Real big for a Mexican."

Beckett said, "All right. Roy Scott went out of here in a taxi, came back in a blue Ford with two Mexicans. He went out again in the Ford, and came back in the Mustang with Stella Ortega. The Ortega girl says she doesn't know who the other two were. You heard the Mustang leave about four A.M. Another car, maybe even the Mustang, came back—maybe a few minutes later, maybe longer. You heard someone walking, but you don't know who, and no one came to the office."

Byers nodded. "I was mostly asleep, but that's how I remember it. I didn't see anyone till the cops woke me up."

"And no one saw you. You were alone here."

Byers licked his lips, but said nothing.

Beckett turned to the day man. "Where were you after you went off duty?"

"I went home and ate," the day man said. "I went to the Beach Tavern till it closed. Then I went home to sleep."

"You're married?"

"I live alone, and it's only a couple blocks from here."

"You know the Ortega girl? Or the other two?"

"No. I've been arrested, if that's what you want. Gambling, mostly. One count of fraud."

"Nice," Beckett said. "The dead man didn't come here by accident. Roy Scott asked him here, or he followed Scott. Or a killer followed one or the other of them."

"Scott walked in alone," the day man said.

"No car following? Watching? Maybe across the road?"

"Not that I saw," the day man said.

"Anyone come around asking for him?"

"I'd have told the cops that," the day man said.

Byers said, "Not when I was on the desk."

"Anyone ask for someone beside Scott? Anyone work to get a look at the register? Maybe came in, but didn't stay?"

Byers was blinking like a startled owl. "There *was* a guy!" he said. "Came in around eight P.M. Right before I asked Scott to tone down the music. He wanted a room, was about to sign the register when he asked me if we had a pool. I told him he'd have seen it on the sign if we had, and we had a whole ocean out back. He said he was afraid of the ocean, and walked out. I forgot him, Mr. Beckett, but he sure saw the register."

"What did he look like?"

"I didn't notice, you know? Dark hair, dark suit. He had a yellow car, though. New. A GM car, I think."

Beckett said, "There's a highway bus stop near, at Dune Drive and the freeway. Maybe a mile and a half."

"That's right," Byers said, "and there's a bus through from L.A. that gets into San Vicente depot at four-fifty P.M. It'd stop at Dune Drive about four-thirty. If Scott walked straight here, he'd make it about five-ten."

Beckett went to the telephone. He called the main bus depot in San Vicente and asked if anyone had come in after 7:00 P.M. last night asking about a soldier on the Los Angeles bus. After he had identified himself, it took fifteen minutes, but he got his answer—a man *had* asked if a sergeant had gotten off the L.A. bus. No soldier had, not that anyone remembered. No one remembered what the man who had asked had looked like, either. Beckett hung up.

"The Dune Drive stop," he said to Byers, "is the only other stop this side of San Vicente besides the depot, right?"

"The only one inside ten miles," Byers said.

"So if Roy Scott was coming to San Vicente," Beckett said, "there was nowhere else he could have left the bus. If anyone had known he was on the bus, it wouldn't have been too hard to find him."

*

Marlene Scott wore a large summer hat as she stepped across the grass toward the small corral. She carried a pair of white gloves. There was loud shouting at the corral. Her husband leaned on the fence beside her younger son, Hamilton. Neither of them noticed Marlene until she was beside them. They were watching the foreman, Jess Rhine, riding the same young horse Hamilton had been working with.

"When you buy a sheriff," Marlene said to her husband, "you should make sure he can't weasel out."

"I didn't buy Hoag," Ben Scott said. "I don't own him."

"Then you wasted a lot of money."

"He can't always favor Roy. No one can."

"Why not? You're an important man. We're important. Roy should be favored."

"Because we're patricians?" Ben Scott said. The small round-faced man looked away across the vast ranchland. "We're not patricians, Marlene. At least, I'm not. Rich, that's all. My father was a dirt-rancher, my grandfather was a cowhand who drifted here with one pair of pants and a saddle. They sent me East to school, made me a businessman, I'm a whiz with a desk. But all that didn't make me an aristocrat. I just look like one, well-mannered and arrogant flab."

"Nostalgia for sagebrush and poverty, Ben?" Marlene said. "Reverting to the saddle and the open fire in your old age? The trouble is, you never were any of that at all."

"Maybe I wish I had been," Ben said, and he turned to watch Jess Rhine on the young horse, a tamed horse now.

"And maybe you still can be," Marlene said. "Why didn't you tell Hoag that Roy's been gone for over two weeks, not two days?"

Ben turned. "Because we don't know where he's been, or what he's done! Now . . . I don't believe he's killed anyone, not Roy—but where is he, Marlene? Where's he gone? Why?"

The dark-haired younger son, Hamilton, spoke for the first time since Marlene had come to the corral. His boyish face was unhappy, accusing. "Roy's crazy, don't you two know that yet?" he said. "I saw it even before that thing with Ted Andrewski, but you wouldn't let them send him to get help, no. Bad for the family image!"

"There's nothing wrong with Roy, Ham," Ben said.

"He was unsettled, yes, but he steadied down, and Hoag agreed that he'd been tricked by Andrewski. He was best at home."

"Sure, he's swell," Hamilton said.

The youth looked away again toward where Jess Rhine and the other men were unsaddling the trembling colt. Marlene began to draw on her long gloves.

Ben Scott watched her. "Where are you going?"

"Town. I have things to do, Ben, and it keeps me busy."

"You've been to town a lot the last month."

"Shopping and errands. My summer wardrobe and the party."

"Just when Roy disappeared?"

Marlene smoothed the gloves over her fingers. "While we're making insinuations, that photo of the dead man Hoag showed us did seem a little familiar. Someone I've seen you with, Ben, perhaps?"

"No," Ben said.

They faced each other in the hot sun across some unspoken barrier. Hamilton watched them with a kind of disgust on his young face. Marlene Scott's eyes went dark as if a cloud had passed over the sun.

"He'll call us," Marlene said. "When he needs us."

"Will he?" Ben said. "Why did he leave, Marlene? Without a word, a note, anything?"

"Funny, I was going to ask you that," she said, and walked away toward the big ranch house.

*

Lee Beckett broke the police seal on unit fifteen at the Sierra Motel. He unlocked the door—and heard the noise inside the unit.

A thump. As if something had struck a wall.

Beckett drew his pistol, went inside crouched with the pistol out in front, jumped to the left inside the door.

The room was a mess. The unmade bed had been pulled apart, the empty canvas suitcase in a corner had been ripped up, drawers were out on the floor, tables and chairs overturned. Closet doors stood open.

No one was in the room.

A rear window was broken, and was open. The curtain hung outside through the open window as if someone had pulled it after him when he climbed out—the thump Beckett had heard.

He ran out and around to the rear of the unit. No one was there, but someone walked on the beach below the clay cliff where the motel stood. Beckett went down the first path behind the motel.

Some fifty yards away up the beach a man walked in the soft sand close to the steep clay cliffs. As Beckett saw him, the man turned toward another path up the dune cliffs, and looked back.

Beckett had a quick glimpse of a young face—thin, almost delicate. A cold, unsmiling face, and two of the hardest eyes he had ever seen. Or that was what Beckett thought he saw in the brief moment before the man turned away again and started up the path from the beach.

A slender, smallish man wearing an expensive-looking dark gray suit and no hat, his thick hair cropped close and neat with military precision, his posture ramrod-straight, his step short and crisp up the path.

"You there! Hold it!" Beckett called out.

The slender man did not look around again. Almost imperceptibly, without haste, he seemed to walk faster up the steep path toward the top of the cliffs. He didn't run.

Beckett ran.

The slender man passed out of sight behind a turn in the path. As he ran, Beckett looked up toward the top of the clay cliff. Another man stood at the edge on top. A bigger man, little more than a bulky shadow at the distance with the sun behind him, his face turned away from Beckett, as if looking out to sea and admiring the view. There was nothing to say that the two men were together, yet Beckett suddenly sensed that if he caught up to the slender young man, the bigger man would be there, too.

He didn't catch the slender man.

He climbed the path as fast as he could, at a panting trot on the steep angle, and came out on the top. The man on the beach was already getting into a black Buick parked on Dune Drive some fifty feet away. He showed no haste —the time, pace and distance necessary to escape Beckett calculated precisely, coolly.

The bigger man was nowhere in sight.

The black Buick pulled away into the morning traffic.

Beckett had no time even to get the license number.

*

Beckett found the bundle of clothes on the beach after an hour of searching. They were medium-priced, chain-store men's clothes stuffed behind rocks at the cliff base near where the path from the Sierra Motel came down to the beach. A brown suit, white shirt, figured brown tie, brown shoes, brown socks, a brown belt. Everything was there except underwear. There was no identification. The labels were all Roos Atkins, California.

Beckett carried the clothes up the path, and went

back into unit fifteen. It had been searched hard but fast, a hasty job by someone looking for more than a missing soldier. From what had been torn open, the way the search had been made at random, Beckett's experienced eye told him that the searcher had no specific item in mind, no known object of a certain size and shape. The searcher had not been exactly sure of what he was looking for.

Beckett searched. He found nothing that seemed important.

In the bathroom there was a toothbrush, toothpaste, shaving cream, after-shave lotion, and a safety razor. Roy Scott had obviously left in a hurry—yet no identification had been left in the unit—not Scott's and not the dead man's. All the towels had been used, as if someone had taken a lot of showers in a short time. More than one person? Or had Roy Scott been preparing himself for suicide? A ritual purification?

In the main room Beckett looked at the record that was still on the small record player the soldier had made such a point of buying. The record was *Invitation to the Dance*, by Von Weber. Beckett started the player, set the needle. A stately introduction filled the room, and then the dance music of a past century.

"Noble," Beckett said aloud, remembering Stella Ortega's story of last night as the vigorous old dance played.

He shut off the machine, and left the unit.

He returned the key to the motel office, then went to his car and drove to the next motel in the direction of where Dune Drive crossed the freeway.

*

It was midafternoon when Beckett parked at the old brick courthouse that was an eyesore to those who wanted revived Spanish architecture in San Vicente. To the descendants of the invading American adventurers who had built it, it was a monument. The battle went on, outweighed only by the price of lemons and land.

The office of the prosecutor was on the second floor. Beckett dropped the clothes he'd found on Charles Tucker's desk, and sat down.

The prosecutor studied the clothes, listened to their story. "They'd fit the dead man, or Roy Scott," he said.

"No matter whose they are," Beckett said, "it means that Roy had civilian clothes with him. Maybe he didn't leave his uniform just on a sudden impulse, Charley."

Tucker thought. "If they are Roy Scott's clothes, he's probably dead, too. Maybe in the sea. Another victim, or a suicide because he killed our dead man. One way or the other, though, if they are Roy's clothes, then someone else took our victim's stuff."

"I don't think they are Roy Scott's clothes," Beckett said. "He doesn't sound like a man who would wear all brown, or buy in a chain store. I think they're the dead man's clothes, and Roy Scott ran in his own civies. In that case, Charley, no one else had to be there. Roy could have stripped the dead guy and hidden the clothes just to confuse the issue."

"I've got his prints and description on all the wires," Tucker said, "but nothing yet. The clothes might help. I'll see what the police lab can do with them."

"See what you can do with some other descriptions, too," Beckett said. He told Tucker about the search of the motel unit, and the two men he had seen on the beach. "Maybe those men on the beach have no connection to the dead man or Roy Scott, but someone is looking for something, Charley."

"There's more than a psycho soldier? What, Lee? The drug angle?"

"Just say maybe we're not the only ones interested in Roy Scott or the dead man. Get the police and Hoag's people on those two descriptions, they should be around town somewhere—and add one more." He explained about the unknown man who had seen the Sierra Motel register and had asked at the bus depot for a sergeant on the Los Angeles bus last night. "I checked the other motels on Dune Drive. Three of them remembered a man who asked for a room about eight P.M. last night, and then changed his mind. Two remember he had a yellow car. No one can describe him."

"He could be one of the two men you saw on the beach."

"He could be," Beckett agreed.

"Any ideas besides drugs, Lee?"

"No," Beckett said. "But Roy Scott was in the army for three years. That's a lot of time, a lot of people, and a lot of places. It could be that if he was thinking about suicide, there was more reason than a psycho whim, and maybe murder solved his problem better."

"Some real problem he couldn't handle? Like someone out to get him one way or another?"

"It's a reason for murder," Beckett said. "A killer usually thinks he's got something very real to gain, Charley."

"Yeh," Charles Tucker said.

*

After Lee Beckett had gone, Prosecutor Charles Tucker leaned back in his desk chair and looked up at the ceiling of his office. It was growing hot in San Vicente. Tucker shut his eyes and didn't move for a full five minutes in the silent office. The clock on his wall ticked loudly.

At last he opened his eyes, reached for his telephone. "Wes? Drop what you're on, turn it over to the other boys. Yes, right now. I want you to start digging into Ben Scott's business deals. Everything you can find. I want to know all that Ben's been working on for the past year."

4

Silver Camp Pass had once been the stagecoach route from northern Buena Costa County to San Vicente. That had been before the freeway was built along the coast, and it had not been so very long ago. There were still old men who came to drink in the bar of the Coach Inn in Santa Ysolde, with its enormous old fireplace where whole trees still burned in winter, who remembered the stagecoaches and the horses straining up the pass.

The pass highway was still the short route into the Santa Ysolde Valley over the mountains, and Lee Beckett drove over it now into the valley of brown wild oats and irrigated green fields. Where the highway came out of the Santa Ysolde range, a secondary road led south into the rough back country. A rugged area of bears, coyotes, abandoned farms, and isolated little communities like the old mining settlement of Silver Camp—a town now of weekend cabins for San Vicente and Santa Ysolde, a few clannish hill families, and the young newcomers seeking a simpler life that was basic and rough but not quite as rough as in the real wilderness of the main Coast Range farther inland.

Beckett did not take the turnoff, but stayed on the main highway through the valley and the German community of Dresden. A few miles before the major village of Santa Ysolde, he turned into a dirt side road. A wooden archway over the side road announced: *The Charro Ranch*. A painted Black Angus bull hung from the archway.

The Charro Ranch was the largest in the county, but small compared to the vast spreads of true cattle country, and land in Buena Costa County was too valuable to use for raising simple market cattle. Instead, the Charro raised prize Black Angus in demand all across the nation for breeding, and blooded horses in equal demand.

A mile from the highway, the sprawling old ranch house of white adobe and red-tiled roofs was set in tall shade trees. There was a single horse barn and a small corral, the main barns and corrals on another part of the ranch. The old adobe house stood off the dirt road at the end of a circular gravel driveway among the trees and gardens of flowers. There was a vast lawn dotted with tables, a swimming pool, and a red-brick patio and barbecue area behind the house.

A Japanese houseman guided Beckett through the mammoth living room, with its incongruous modern furniture, and out to the patio. A small man dressed in the riding jeans, western shirt, boots and Stetson of a rancher came to greet Beckett.

"Mr. Beckett? I'm Ben Scott. You have news?"

"No news, Mr. Scott," Beckett said.

The rancher's shoulders sagged, and his fifty-five years showed on his worried face. A round indoor face with quick eyes behind horn-rimmed glasses, the soft belly and hands of a man who had lived his life behind a desk. A businessman, despite the western riding clothes—a rich and modern rancher.

"Where is he, Mr. Beckett?" Ben Scott said, chewed on his lip. Then he seemed to remember that he wasn't alone. "I'm sorry. This is my wife, Marlene, Mr. Beckett, and that's my other boy, Hamilton."

The small, slim blond woman sat at the edge of the pool in a one-piece black bathing suit with no back and little front. Beckett's experienced eye told him that she was past forty, if not by much, but was a long way from being resigned and ready to relax to quiet years. Her eyes were bright and appraising, her mind seeming to be more on Beckett than on his reason for being there. The thick-shouldered youth, Hamilton Scott, stood on the diving board, and dove as Beckett watched. The woman, Marlene Scott, looked toward her second son, and her mind came back to who Beckett was.

"You haven't found Roy?" she said. "Or heard?"

"Only some clothes. A brown suit from Roos Atkins."

The young man, Hamilton, climbed from the pool. His face had a certain stallion emptiness. The kind of popular young man who would find books and theories a mystery all his life.

"Roy never had a suit in his life," Hamilton said.

Beckett nodded, but he was watching the wife. Marlene Scott was like sleek, expensive crystal. A smooth piece of fine art looking for—what? Something more. Restless.

She said, "I know that Roy couldn't have—" She stopped, rubbed her hands along her slim thighs. "It's terrible to think of him out there alone somewhere, afraid. Why doesn't he come home? We've always helped him. We have to give an important party. How can I get ready with Roy—"

"There won't be any party, damn it," Ben Scott said.

Marlene shook her head. "We can't cancel now. A lot of people are here from out of the county just to attend."

"For God sake, Marlene, he's your son!"

"All right," she said. "But how do we help him by dropping everything? What can we do anyway? This is an important party, nothing's changed. Martin Elder came all the way from New York."

"What the hell do I care about Elder?" Ben Scott snapped.

"Business doesn't mean anything now, Ben?" Marlene said. "All right, but if we cancel the party, we'll have to say why."

Ben Scott said nothing. Beckett made a noise. They all looked at him.

"Did any of you know Stella Ortega before?" he said.

"The girl who says she was with him?" Ben Scott said. "No, I never heard him mention her."

"Or anyone like her," Marlene Scott said.

"She says she knew him before he went to the army."

"He was a boy then," Marlene said. "A wild boy."

Ben Scott looked toward the small corral. "I suppose he was spoiled. Drinking, chasing, doing what his whim wanted, never home, arrogant. Maybe we lived too much the same way ourselves. I remember one of his high school teachers told me that Roy had no direction. Once the teacher assigned a class essay about future goals, and Roy asked how you spelled 'Masserati.' ''

"He flunked out of two colleges," Marlene Scott said. "When he actually graduated from the university here, we were as surprised as we were pleased."

"I hoped he'd come into the business then, but he went into the army!" Ben Scott said. "I could have gotten him deferred, gotten him started."

"He enlisted?" Beckett said. "That's unusual these days."

"To spite us," Marlene said. "To defy me."

"He made quite a record," Ben Scott said, a puzzled pride in his voice. "Twelve medals, including a Silver Star. Wounded, too. In hospital in Japan before he was discharged."

Hamilton Scott said, "Psycho! It was battle fatigue."

"If it was, he was over it!" Ben Scott snapped.

Beckett said, "Did he ever talk about suicide?"

"Of course not," Marlene Scott said.

"No," Ben Scott said.

Hamilton said, "He did to me. I tried to tell Ben and Mother he was sick, irrational, but they never listened."

The generation gap opened like a fissure on the patio.

"All right, we'd been told he was shaken up," Ben Scott said uneasily. "But when he got home, I saw nothing wrong. He was changed, yes—for the better! He was quieter, older, more mature. A little detached maybe, but grown up. He went right to work in my real estate management office, settled down."

Beckett said, "You make it sound like he'd been home a long time?"

"Six months," Ben Scott said. "Long enough to know—"

"Six months? Then why was he in uniform last night?"

They looked at each other.

Hamilton said, "Roy took the uniform off the day he came home."

"He put it on again. He's in civilian clothes now, but he wore the uniform last night."

"I didn't know he even had it with him," Ben Scott said.

"With him? Where?"

They were all silent. Ben Scott was looking away toward the small corral again.

Marlene moved her feet in the pool water. She looked up at her husband. "Ben?"

The businessman-rancher continued to stare into the distance. "Hoag didn't mention anything about suicide. Do you think Roy might be suicidal, Mr. Beckett?"

"He could be. Stella Ortega thought he was."

Ben Scott shivered. "We don't know where Roy's been, Mr. Beckett. I told Hoag he left here a few days ago, that was a lie. He left two weeks ago. We don't know why, or to where, and we didn't know he'd come back."

Beckett said, "We don't buy all of the Ortega girl's story, at least some of it's a lie, but she said that Roy talked about talking to his father, and she'd have no reason to make that up."

A silence rested heavy on the sunny patio. Ben Scott

was watching a turkey vulture soar high in the clear sky now. Hamilton was scowling.

Marlene Scott rubbed her legs. "Perhaps he didn't mean Ben, Mr. Beckett," she said. "Ben is Roy's stepfather, I was married before. Roy's father still lives in San Vicente—Howard Sill, 209 West Padre Street."

"Was Roy close to his real father?"

Marlene squeezed her thighs. "I divorced Howard Sill over twenty years ago. I haven't spoken to him since the first year after, and I didn't think Roy had. Ben is his legal father, he took Ben's name long ago, I'd have said he didn't even know Howard."

Beckett said, "He vanished two weeks ago, came back to a motel, saw friends you don't know, talked about his father—maybe the real father he hardly knew. He sounds like a man with a lot on his mind to me. What could be bothering him?"

Marlene Scott said, "Honestly, Mr. Beckett, we don't—"

"Why don't you tell him about that car!" Hamilton cried.

"What car?"

"Roy and a guy he'd known in Vietnam burned a car for the insurance money!" Hamilton said.

Ben Scott said, "The other boy was paid to burn the car! Roy was duped, fooled into it. Hoag made no charges."

"When was this?"

"About a month ago," Ben Scott said. "It can't have any connection. Roy was exonerated completely."

"Who was the other man?"

"Ted Andrewski," Hamilton said. "A pothead lives down on the beach."

"Pothead? Did Roy use drugs?"

"Of course not!" Marlene said.

"He played around with them," Hamilton said.

The generation gap widened into an abyss in the sun. Beckett seemed to think for a time. So did the Scotts.

Beckett said, "Did Roy ever talk about trouble while he was in the army? Anything special? Was he ever scared, worried?"

This time they all shook their heads.

Ben Scott was following the soaring flight of the vulture again. "You raise a boy to see what you see," the rancher said, "and then he sees something else. You suddenly don't know who he is, then you don't know where he is, and I'm not sure that there's much you can do. But I want you to find him, Mr. Beckett, no matter what he's done."

"If he's done anything," Marlene said. "I don't believe he has. It's all some mistake, I'm sure of that."

"Maybe it is," Beckett said.

Hamilton dove into the pool, began to swim with long, powerful strokes as if he had to burn up his anger or fear.

*

The Buena Costa County sheriff's office was on the first floor of the jail wing of the courthouse.

"So you'll work for Tucker," Sheriff John Hoag said as Beckett walked into the office, "but not for me."

"He'll let me work without handcuffs," Beckett said.

Hoag's face was neutral. "I'll watch how you work."

"If Roy Scott's guilty, I'll be sure I can prove it," Beckett said. "You forgot to mention that arson Roy was mixed in."

"Maybe because officially he wasn't mixed in it."

"Is that how it's going to be? Just so I'll know. You're off the case, except you'll protect Roy Scott?"

Hoag swiveled in his chair. "A kid named Ted Andrewski got paid to burn a car for the insurance. He botched his getaway, and when we caught him Roy Scott was with him. Roy said it was a prank they'd pulled together. But we got a confession from the car owner—he'd hired Andrewski, he never heard of Roy. I decided that Roy had been tricked, that's all. I figured the war had shaken him, so I turned him over to his folks without even booking him. He needed his family, not jail."

"What happened to Ted Andrewski?"

"Arson charge. We had the owner's confession, and Andrewski had the money he was paid in his house."

"Where's Andrewski now?"

"Who knows? Ask Tucker, he prosecuted."

"Our dead man isn't Andrewski, is he, Hoag?"

"Hell, no."

"Where did Andrewski live at the time?"

"On Delmar Lane, near the beach."

Beckett said, "Both veterans, both said they burned the car. Andrewski gets charged, and Roy goes home."

"We had evidence on Andrewski. Roy had a family, Andrewski didn't. The judge saw the difference, if you don't."

"Everyone's equal before the law," Beckett said, "but some people, like Scotts, are more equal than others, Sheriff?"

Hoag didn't even change expression.

Beckett stood up. "Maybe you let the wrong one go free," he said.

5

The house at 209 West Padre where Howard Sill lived was small behind a narrow lawn. The walk to the door was bordered with massed ranunculus. A woman answered Beckett's ring. She was tall and thin in a cotton dress. She had to be about Marlene Scott's age, the early forties, but there the resemblance ended. This woman's hair was gray, her face was worn thin, and she looked ten years older than Marlene Scott.

"Howard's not home yet," she said. "Is it about a car? Come in. I'm Mrs. Sill. I'm sure Howard won't be long."

"It's about his son, Mrs. Sill," Beckett said.

"Roy Scott?" Her eagerness faded, and her voice went flat. "I see. You can wait in the living room then."

The living room was small and clean, with nondescript furniture neither good nor bad. When Beckett was in the room, the woman walked away to some other part of the house without asking anything, as if Roy Scott's name removed her from the scene.

It was past six o'clock when a pale-faced man with narrow shoulders came into the house. There was a tonsure of dark hair around his bald crown, and his brown suit was limp. He walked as if his legs hurt.

"You want to see me?" he said.

"That's right, Mr. Sill. Lee Beckett, from the county prosecutor's office. I want to talk about Roy Scott."

"Prosecutor?" Howard Sill said. "About Roy?"

"Have you seen him recently, Mr. Sill?"

"No, why should I? Talk to Ben Scott."

"Did you see Roy last night?" Beckett asked.

Sill began to take off his jacket. "No."

Beckett said, "It looks like Roy planned suicide last night. He told someone he wanted to talk to his father. Only it turned into murder instead. Now he's missing."

"Suicide? Last night? Murder?" Howard Sill said each phrase slowly, separately, as if listening to their sound. He hung his jacket in a closet, called to his wife, "Sybil? Can I have a beer?"

He sat down in a yellow plastic lounge chair. "I hadn't seen Roy, except on the street at a distance, for over twenty years, Mr. Beckett. The Scotts have no use for me. About three weeks ago Roy showed up here. Just walked in. He seemed shaky. He wanted to talk, but we had nothing to talk about."

"What did he want to talk about?"

"The world. That's too much for me to chew on. I'm high school, and TV sports on Sunday. I think I'm the backbone of the country, but I can't argue about it. If my world is wrong, I don't know it, and I couldn't change myself anyway."

"This was three weeks ago?"

"Yep. He came twice. One day he talked about the Scotts being the whole world, and acted real bitter. The next time he just sat around watching Sybil and me."

"Depressed?" Beckett said. "Angry?" ·

"Both. He said he'd been sick, but he got better, only maybe getting better was being sicker. Not much sense in it."

Sill's wife came in with a glass of beer. She stood over Howard Sill. Neither of them offered Beckett a beer.

"Was he afraid? Had anything happened in the last month? Did he use any names?" Beckett asked.

"No on all of that," Sill said.

"Dr. Remak," Mrs. Sill said. "He talked about a Dr. Remak. I remember because I thought he needed a doctor."

"Who is Dr. Remak?"

"How would we know?" Mrs. Sill said.

Beckett looked at Howard Sill. "What do you do, Sill?"

"Used-car salesman. I've sold most everything in my time."

Mrs. Sill said, "What do you care what Howard does? Why don't you bother the Scotts? What's Roy Scott to us?"

Beckett got up. "All right. But if Roy contacts you, tell me. I'm telling you, understand?"

Sill nodded, and the wife glared. Beckett went out to his car. He used the radio to call Tucker's office. The prosecutor was out, and the last address the office had for Ted Andrewski was 9 Delmar Lane.

*

From the front window, Howard Sill watched Beckett talking into the radio in his official car.

"You think he knows more than he let on, Syb?" Sill said.

Sybil Sill sat on the couch. "Marlene took that boy from you when he was three. It's not our concern."

Sill watched Beckett drive off. "He's my son, Syb."

"He's Ben Scott's son. Let Ben Scott suffer. We've had our share. She could have helped you."

"I never asked her, Syb."

"Because you knew what her answer would have been. You're a good salesman, you needed a break. Now let the Scotts solve their own problem. We've got ourselves to take care of."

Howard Sill nodded, drank his beer.

*

Number 9 Delmar Lane was a shack at the edge of the beach. An orange Lotus with racing stripes sat in the driveway. As Beckett walked to the shack, he saw a girl on the sand behind it. She had long dark hair that blew in the late evening sun. When she heard Beckett, she turned and stared at his car with its police aerial. Beckett walked up to her.

"You're the detective?" she said.

Her face was small and boyish, but the rest of her was neither small nor boyish. Her legs were long in a mini-skirt; her breasts and hips were full. A young animal balanced on the edge of the future.

48

"What detective were you expecting?" Beckett said.

"The one looking for Roy Scott. I'm Janice Rhine. My dad works at the Charro—ranch foreman. I've known Roy all my life. I'm going to marry Ham. He's inside the shack."

"Why?" Beckett said.

"To find his brother," Janice Rhine said. She drew some stick-figures in the sand. "Did Roy kill that man? Really?"

"I don't know. What do you think?"

She shrugged, but only after she seemed to think about it. "How would I know? He was fun before he went to Vietnam."

"Spoiled and arrogant?"

She thought again. "The Scotts would say that, I guess. Most adults would. Because he didn't do what they expected."

"Like take drugs, flunk out of colleges? All fun?"

"I never saw him use drugs. He dropped out of the colleges because they didn't give him anything. He used to say they never showed him what ways there were, what *choices* he had. He didn't want just what he was told to want, like me."

"You want what you're supposed to want, Janice?"

"Roy said I do, when he came home. I guess he's right. He was always *looking*. I thought he'd found what he wanted at the university, but maybe he's still looking."

"What did he find at the university?"

"Who knows? He mixed with the militants then, got serious. He had some strange friends off-campus, too. He never talked to me about it, I was just a kid."

"You know any names of the strange friends off-campus?"

"No. It was three years ago anyway. After he came home he never went around with anyone I could see. Always alone."

Beckett said, "Militants are usually anti-army, and anti-war. How did Roy happen to enlist three years ago?"

"I don't know. I remember he had a big fight with Marlene about it, but all he said was he had to see for himself."

"See what, Janice?"

"The war, I guess. The army. The Communists, maybe."

"What else did he say when he came back?"

"We didn't talk much. I had Ham, you know? Roy was pretty quiet, until that car thing a month ago."

"Did he say why he burned that car?"

"No, not to me," Janice said. "All he said to me was that he wanted to be sent away. I told him he was crazy." She looked up at Beckett. "I guess he is a little crazy, you know? I mean, coming back here to a motel and all. Hiding out."

"Maybe he is," Beckett said. "Who's Ham inside with?"

"Ted Andrewski's girl." She stood up, brushed the sand from her young thighs. "I'll go inside with you."

The shack was dim and bare. A single table, two chairs, and a mattress on the floor. Hamilton Scott stood over a girl who sat on the mattress. She wore a long, shapeless dress, and looked up at Janice Rhine with scorn. Janice put her arms around Hamilton Scott, smiled up at him.

"I thought maybe Roy would come here," Hamilton said to Beckett. "I didn't know where Andrewski was."

"Where is he?" Beckett said.

The girl on the mattress said, "Everyone's worried about Ted. *They* got trouble, so now they worry about Ted."

"You're Andrewski's girl?" Beckett said.

"His *wife,* mister! All legal. It didn't help us. You want to know where Ted is? The funny farm! The nut house!" The girl on the mattress closed her eyes, rocked. "They count bodies in Nam. What about the dead still walking around? Who counts them? Who cares? They come home and the bands play, only home is a psycho ward. File them and forget them. If they went off anti-war, they come home zombies. If they went off waving the flag, they come home maniacs calling everyone Communists. What happens to the wives? We don't have men, we've got sick children who don't know who or what they are."

Beckett said, "Maybe I can help. Where is Ted?"

The girl lay back on the mattress, her eyes still closed. "Help? You mean help Roy Scott. Everyone comes here to help Roy Scott. What do I care about Roy Scott?"

"Someone else was here looking for Roy Scott?" Beckett said.

"On Saturday. Blond guy. Some square."

"What was his name?"

"I didn't ask, he didn't tell. He didn't care about Ted."

"What did you tell him?"

"What I told Handsome there with the square chick —I don't know about Roy Scott, and Ted's under the rug." She opened her eyes, looked at Beckett. "Maybe Ted's safer where he is. He can't hurt himself or anyone else any more."

Hamilton Scott said, "Ted's at the John Blake Veterans' Hospital, Mr. Beckett. She told me."

The girl on the mattress laughed. "I wonder who the hell John Blake was? Now there's a real honor, right? A crazy house named after you. He must have been a general."

*

Hamilton Scott sat behind the wheel of the sleek orange Lotus. Janice Rhine was close beside him, held his arm.

"He's my brother, Mr. Beckett," Hamilton said. "He's been funny since he came home. I mean, he sat in the office doing nothing! Wasting his chances. I should have known he was bad."

"Drugs maybe, Ham?" Beckett said.

"I don't know. I never used drugs, I don't know what they do to you. Anyway, I guess Roy was always unstable, you know?"

"You mean even before the army and Vietnam?"

Hamilton nodded. Janice Rhine squeezed the muscular boy's arm. She looked at Beckett outside the sleek car.

"Mr. Beckett," she said, "the day Roy left two weeks ago, he sent me a poem. I never showed it to anyone except Ham. I didn't think it was important, but maybe it is."

She opened her bag, took out an envelope, gave it to Beckett. There was a small clipping inside. Beckett read it aloud:

"Oh nobody's a long time
 Nowhere's a big pocket
 To put little
 Pieces of nice things that
 Have never really happened
 To anyone except
 Those people who were lucky enough
 Not to get born."

Janice Rhine said, "It's by Kenneth Patchen. He's an old man now, he wrote that a long time ago."

"Not much is new," Beckett said, give her back the poem.

He went to his own car. When he looked back, Janice Rhine had her head on Hamilton's chest. They were like a single statue, young and vulnerable. Not lost, but not yet found.

*

Over his restaurant dinner, Beckett reworked the case so far step by step. The blond man who had asked Ted Andrewski's girl about Roy Scott, and had been told where Andrewski was, sounded like the dead man at the Sierra Motel, and Roy sounded more and more suicidal—but where had it changed to murder, and why? There were too many empty spaces. After his coffee Beckett went out to try to fill in one space.

There were two taxi companies in San Vicente. The Yellow Cab Company had made no pickups the night before at the Sierra. The San Vicente Taxi Corporation had—one at 5:32 P.M. to the King Discount store, and one at 8:30 P.M. to a busy corner in the slums. The driver didn't know where Roy Scott had gone from the taxi.

Beckett made the rounds of the bars and restaurants in the area. No one admitted seeing an army sergeant. No one recognized the descriptions of the two Mexican-Americans who had been at the Sierra with Roy Scott. It was an area where people minded their own business, and knew a useless description when they heard one. They would admit nothing until Beckett had more to go on. No one seemed to have seen Stella Ortega last night, either.

At midnight Beckett gave up. He drove to Charles Tucker's house. There was still light in a downstairs room. Tucker came to the door, took Beckett into a study.

"Anything, Charley?" Beckett asked.

"No. It looks like our dead man has no record of any kind, and if your men on the beach are here, they're being careful."

"I figured they would be," Beckett said. "You didn't tell me that Ben Scott isn't Roy's real father."

"Is that important, Lee?"

"All of a sudden Roy visited his real father after twenty years and more. Why, Charley?"

Tucker sat on his desk. "Ben Scott isn't the father of either boy. Marlene married Howard Sill in high school. She divorced him when Roy was three, married a man who worked for Ben Scott, had Hamilton fast, and met Ben. She dumped Ham's father, he left town, and she married Ben. The boys took Ben's name legally; everyone thinks of them as Ben's sons."

"Except, maybe, Roy Scott. A picture's shaping, Charley. Roy came home quiet, went to work for Ben, had no trouble until a month ago he mixed up in a stupid arson. Hoag let him off, while you prosecuted Ted Andrewski fast. That same week Roy went to his real father—depressed and angry. He gave Janice Rhine a suicidal poem, and vanished. Two weeks later he's back, acting like he means to kill himself with a rope, but another man is killed. Why? What happened to make him run away? I think I better talk to Ted Andrewski, Charley."

"The John Blake Hospital is just north of Los Angeles," Tucker said. "Ask for Dr. Emil Remak, he's treating Andrewski."

"Remak?" Beckett said. "Who is Dr. Remak?"

"A former army psychiatrist who treated Andrewski in Japan. That's why we committed Andrewski to him. Why?"

Beckett said, "Roy Scott was hospitalized in Japan, and he knows Dr. Remak, Charley."

6

Dr. Emil Remak got up twenty minutes early that Wednesday, and drove through the morning fog to the bus stop on Highway 1. He bought the early newspapers, then drove his gray Lincoln back to his new house above the now invisible Pacific.

His wife had breakfast ready. Remak turned the pages of the newspapers as he ate. His wife watched him.

"Is something wrong, Emil?" she asked, sipped her coffee.

"One of my patients walked out two days ago, Phyl, and I'm worried."

"He'll come back," Phyllis Remak said. "They always do."

Remak looked up. "That's a hell of a thing to say. The poor bastards. Worse than the dead."

"They always do come back, Emil—somewhere.

You're a fine doctor, but you can't do miracles, not in that place. The government washes its hands of the bad cases—less battle fatigue than in Korea, they say, forget it. The bad cases were always unstable, they say. What can you do, Emil?"

"I can try, Phyl."

"You tried in Japan. The government doesn't care."

"I'm best here for now, Phyl, we agreed."

"Let's go East, a good hospital. Do the work you can do."

Remak laid the papers aside. "Look, Phyl, we decided, yes? No one pays a thirty-year-old psychiatrist much until he has a reputation or a lot of experience. A VA hospital is the best experience. When I leave, I want a top hospital, and the top dollar, right?"

"We don't need money, Emil."

Remak looked out the kitchen window at the fog that was beginning to lift as the morning warmed. "Give it another year, Phyl. When I'm in charge of the section."

She smiled. "I suppose you know best, Emil."

Remak went back to his newspapers. Phyllis Remak sipped at her coffee and continued to watch him for a time.

"Emil?" she said. "Is there anything special about this one patient? You've had patients leave you before."

"He was one of my patients in Vietnam and Japan."

Phyllis Remak finished her coffee in silence.

*

Lee Beckett saw the hospital wreathed in the thinning fog high above the highway. Bare and massive, like a giant pillbox, it stood on a raw hill a mile up an arid canyon from the sea, with no other buildings near it.

Beckett found an empty space in the parking lot, and joined hordes of doctors and staff hurrying into the building as the day began. A nurse sat at the desk of the psychiatric section.

"Dr. Remak? Yes, your name?"

"Lee Beckett. From San Vicente."

She worked an interoffice telephone. "He'll be out in a minute. He's lost a patient, a voluntary. He hates that, makes him feel he's failed. I figure the voluntaries have to be twice as nutty as the committed—they *ask* to come here."

Beckett sat down to wait. Five minutes passed before a dark-haired man of about thirty came up to Beckett. He wore a white coat, and his eyes were harried.

"Mr. Beckett? I'm Dr. Remak. You're from San Vicente?"

"That means something to you, Doctor?"

"Yes, it does," Remak said. "I lost a patient from there."

The nurse said, "Shall I call his parents yet, Doctor?"

"I'll tell you when, damn it!" Remak snapped.

"But we have to notify—"

"He's twenty-five, Miss Schader. He came here on his own, he's his own responsibility. We'll notify the family when I think we should!" Then Remak softened. "We give them a chance to return on their own, Miss Schader. A sense of self is part of their problem."

"I'm sorry, Doctor," the nurse said.

Remak nodded. "Come into my office, Mr. Beckett."

In the small office, Dr. Remak sat behind his desk. Beckett took a chair facing him.

"You were talking about Roy Scott, Dr. Remak?" Beckett said.

"Yes. You're from the family? Has something happened?"

"I'm from the Buena Costa County prosecutor's office. Yesterday morning we found a man hanging in a motel room. Roy took the room Monday night. He—"

Dr. Remak sat up. "Dead? A suicide?"

Beckett rubbed his chin. "The man was dead, yes."

"Ahhhhhh," Remak let out a breath. "I've been afraid. Damn, damn! I've watched the papers. The waste!"

"Roy Scott was suicidal, Doctor?"

Remak nodded. "I saw it, but there wasn't time. Twice we talked about it straight out. He was so damned rational! Once he said, 'Why not, Doc, all you do is go on paying rent and taxes for an empty room in a bloody world. It's the world that's suicidal, Doc. I'll be saving trouble.' What could I tell him?"

"That dead men can't change anything."

"He was at the point of thinking nothing could ever be changed anyway."

"So he wouldn't dance the tune," Beckett said.

"Dance? So he left a note? Said that?" Remak sighed. "He had an abstract mind. All symbols and metaphors, hard to fight. He played a record over and over in our rec room—Weber's *Invitation to the Dance*. It's gone. I suppose he took it."

"It was in the room," Beckett said. "When did he come here?"

"About two weeks ago. He walked in one morning, said he came to talk to me. I was his doctor in Saigon and

Japan, you see. I'd thought he was one of my successful efforts, almost normal when he was discharged. You never know, Mr. Beckett."

"Almost normal, Doctor?"

"About all we can hope for in the mental problems wars produce. War is a traumatic shock to many young men, especially this Vietnam one. On the one hand it's the most savage, relentless war, and on the other there are doubts it should ever have happened or can be won. When he went home Roy seemed at least stable. Two weeks ago he was much more disturbed, even agitated."

"The way he was when you first had him over there?"

"Not exactly." Remak thought about it. "Over there he was in shock from the war itself, from Vietcong terror against civilians, from our own terror tactics, from the corruption he felt he'd seen in Saigon. Two weeks ago he was disturbed more by the *motives* he saw behind it all, the world as he saw it. Over there he couldn't accept how wrong it all was. Two weeks ago he didn't care about right or wrong."

Remak shook his head. "In Japan he wasn't suicidal. The opposite—a crusader for right. Two weeks ago he felt that there *was* no right, no difference between right and wrong. Even between people. He talked in wild extremes. His stepfather was the same as a Saigon politician. His mother was a Vietcong. Like that."

"Did he mention arson on a car in San Vicente?"

"Yes, but I can't discuss that. It happens that the other man involved is a patient here, too. One of mine."

"Ted Andrewski's still here?"

"Yes," Remak said. "I can say one thing—when Roy

talked of the arson, he talked about everyone wanting to grab, cheat, and steal. *Everyone.* So it must be right, the right way to live, and so it was right to help anyone grab or steal."

"Did Roy and Andrewski ever meet here?"

"Often. They were friends. I believe, in group therapy for common problems. Why? You think that Ted had something to do with Roy's suicide? I doubt that he—"

"I didn't say Roy was dead, Doctor. I said we found a man hanging in Roy's room. It wasn't Roy."

*

Dr. Emil Remak leaned back in his chair. He breathed hard. He sat with one hand across his eyes. "A trick? Why?"

"No trick," Beckett said. "I said we found a man hanging. You assumed it was Roy. It was an edge, I took it. To see what you'd say thinking he was dead."

Remak lowered his hand. "You thought I might not tell the truth if I thought he was alive? What did you learn by it?"

"That you really think he's suicidal. I've got a story that makes it seem that he was planning suicide, but I wasn't sure the witnesses were telling the truth. Maybe they are."

"What does Roy say about it? Why did the other man kill himself in Roy's room? Who was the man?"

"We don't have Roy, Doctor, we don't know who the dead man was, and it wasn't suicide, it was murder."

"Murder? Roy killed the man?"

"You think Roy killed him? Is Roy homicidal, too?"

Remak stared. "Don't you know who killed the man?"

"No, we don't."

"Then you have to find Roy! His reason is balanced on a hair. If he killed anyone, he's a time bomb to kill again!"

"That's why I came here, Doctor. To find Roy."

"If I knew where he was, I'd have gone after him."

"Would you? What kind of car do you drive?"

"A gray Continental. Why?"

"Just a thought. Would Andrewski know where Roy might go?"

"I doubt it."

"Can I talk to him?"

Remak frowned. "Ted's in a depressive state. He doesn't have Roy's intelligence or education. A simple man who only wants to be like everyone else. His thoughts confuse him, make him doubt himself. He's hard to reach."

"I can try," Beckett said.

"Yes, all right," Remak said. He picked up the inter-office telephone, spoke to someone in the ward, and hung up. "He's not in the ward, but we can find him. It's a locked ward. Remember, these men have been ground up by horror and opposing theories in Vietnam. They feel like freaks, ashamed. You have to handle them gently."

"I'll remember, Doctor," Beckett said.

*

Dr. Remak unlocked the door that blocked the corridor, and led Beckett into a ward section of the first floor.

"Roy wasn't in this section, Doctor?" Beckett asked.

"No. In an open ward on the second floor. Voluntary."

In the ward where Ted Andrewski had his bed, one

man was reading; the rest slept, or stared up with nothing to do but try to remember that they had once been alive.

"Andrewski's in water therapy," the reading man said. "The bastard always takes longer'n he's supposed to."

The water-therapy room was at the rear of the wing. It was deserted except for a man who sat up to his neck in the whirlpool bath; he had a thin face under black hair.

"That's Andrewski," Remak said low. "Good morning, Ted."

The man in the whirlpool didn't answer. Beckett walked to the bath. Ted Andrewski seemed to watch him all the way, staring at Beckett from the swirling water. Beckett stood over the bath. "Doc!"

Remak was beside him. "What—?"

Under the swirling water, Ted Andrewski's arms hung limp, floating like seaweed.

"My God!" Dr. Remak whispered.

Beckett bent down, felt around the neck of the man in the swirling bath. "A cord around his neck. Tightened with a metal rod like a garrote. The cord's hung on the faucet to hold his head up. He's still warm. Not too long. He . . . Doc?"

Remak shrank back and away. He was trembling.

"You going to be sick?" Beckett said.

Remak nodded, then shook his head, "I don't know. I—"

"Get a hold, Doc," Beckett snapped. "Is that door we came through in the corridor the only way into the section? Quick!"

Remak passed his hand over his face, took deep breaths. "There's a rear door. It should be locked. That's all . . . No, there's the freight entrance into the storeroom where—"

Beckett ran out into the corridor. He saw an orderly. "Dr. Remak needs help in the water room! Where's the rear door?"

"Down the corridor, left," the orderly said.

Beckett ran along the corridor. The rear door was locked and barred inside. Beckett stopped another orderly. "Freight entrance! Where is it?"

"That way. You'll see the storeroom."

Beckett found the storeroom. It was a large concrete-floored room piled with crates and boxes. Four men in work clothes turned to look at Beckett as he ran in. Light streamed into the room through a wide opening that led out to a dock where a truck was being unloaded.

*

Beckett stood on the wide parking lot in the sunlight that had now broken through the fog. People walked everywhere.

The workmen unloading the truck remembered seeing a lot of men in white hospital clothes—and remembered no one special. Maybe someone had come through the storage room, and maybe not. It was hard to say, they had been working. Maybe someone had gone in past them, or come out, or both. Maybe not.

Beckett let his eyes rove across all the people walking near the hospital and the parking lot. There was no way of knowing if any of them had murdered Ted Andrewski.

*

Captain Deraita, Los Angeles sheriff's office, sat in Dr. Emil Remak's office with Remak and Beckett.

"Andrewski died only ten or fifteen minutes before you found him. No one saw anyone suspicious. We found a white doctor's coat outside near the freight entrance."

"The killer knew the hospital," Beckett said.

Dr. Remak sat shaken. "Roy Scott knows the hospital."

Deraita looked at Beckett. "You're already after this Roy Scott?"

"Yes," Beckett said, and explained what had happened in San Vicente. "Maybe someone knew I was about to talk to Ted Andrewski. I could have been followed, or spotted."

"Could be," Captain Deraita said. "Anyone else who might want him dead, Dr. Remak? You were pretty close to him."

Remak shook his head. "He'd cut himself off, massively withdrawn. He had no visitors except his wife twice, and he wouldn't talk to her. He said she was a Communist agent."

"We'll check on where she is," Deraita said.

Beckett said, "But Andrewski did talk to Roy?"

"Yes, often," Remak said. "I don't know what about."

"You've got plenty of resident psychos," Deraita said. "Any one of them could have flipped out."

"Possibly," Remak admitted. "Ted had neither enemies nor friends here, except, of course, Roy Scott."

"You think Roy killed him, Doctor?" Beckett said.

Remak's face was gray now. "Who else could have? Roy is running, hiding, isn't he? It seems he's already killed one man. He could have followed you here. Ted might have known plans Roy had, involvements. Perhaps only where Roy would hide. Or maybe the motive behind

Roy's actions—if there is any motive beyond simple psychosis."

"Did Andrewski ever hint he knew anything about Roy?" Beckett said.

"No, he didn't to me," Remak said.

"How about Roy Scott himself?" Deraita said. "You talked to him a lot, right? What was on his mind? Did he talk about Andrewski? Have anything against him?"

"No," Remak said. "He talked about his family mostly. Not hating them, or angry, but rather . . . fatalistic, yes. They were what they were, and there was no hope. He said once that his mother was an idol who rose naked from the sea like Venus, only that in her case the sea was an expensive private swimming pool, and someone had already bought her body."

"That's all pretty abstract," Captain Deraita said. "What can we do with that?"

Remak ran both hands through his dark hair. "I can't be sure. Roy is an intellectual type who sees everything whole, in symbols, but I had an impression that his parents had done something. Something specific, and recently."

"Done what? When?" Beckett said.

"I don't know what, but I got the idea that it was sudden, a shock, and not too long before he came here two weeks ago. Something Roy considered very bad." Remak looked at both the detectives. "You understand that Roy isn't rational. What he considered very bad could be something trivial or normal."

"He talked about no one else?" Beckett asked.

"His fiancée a few times. A girl named Janice Rhine."

"You mean Hamilton Scott's fiancée," Beckett said.

"No, Roy's. I remember he used to write her sometimes from Japan. He was detached about her this time,
but he was detached about everyone. Everything was sym-
bol and paradox. He said his real father was a failure, and
that perhaps failure was really success. He said getting better was getting worse. He talked of some women he knew,
Stella Ortega and Helen Sanchez. Victims, he called them.
He said they were real and honest because they were victims who stole and dreamed."

"Helen Sanchez?" Beckett said. "You're sure of
that?"

"Yes. He said he had to apologize to them. Does it
mean anything, Mr. Beckett?"

"It means something," Beckett said, and stood up.

"Keep me filled in, Beckett, okay?" Captain Deraita
said. "Meanwhile, I'll work here on the hospital people. I'll
be as quiet as possible, Dr. Remak."

"Yes, thank you," Dr. Remak said, hesitated. "I
might have been able to help Roy if he'd let me, but now I
have to warn both of you. If Roy's killed anyone, he could
be very dangerous. You should be careful, and go armed. I
mean it."

"We'll be careful, Doc," Deraita said.

Beckett was already on his way out.

7

The CasNoir Club, in the slums of San Vicente, was a yellow-brick building without windows in the middle of a parking lot. A black and yellow sign announced: *Topless —Jo Hirsch and The Orcas—No Cover.* The parking lot had two other cars in it in the early afternoon as Beckett parked.

The bartender's eyes retreated into his Indian face when he saw Beckett enter.

Beckett sat at the dim bar. "Hello, Nevés."

"You want a drink, Mr. Beckett?"

"A beer. You've heard I'm working again, Nevés?"

"I heard," the bartender said, set the beer down.

"Still running your game in the back?"

The bartender said nothing.

"Gambling's not my job," Beckett said. "I'm looking for Helen Sanchez. You know where she's living now?"

"I ain't seen her, Mr. Beckett."

"Was she in last night? With a soldier? Sold him some sticks of marijuana?"

"Nobody sells in here."

"But the soldier was in?"

The bartender mopped his face. "A gringo sergeant was in."

"With Helen Sanchez?"

"I don' know. Like I said, I didn't see Helen awhile," the bartender said, sweating now, unsure of what he had said.

"Where's she living?"

"Over Salsipuedes Street, one-forty."

"Who's her man now?"

"Listen, Mr. Beckett, I don' want no trouble with—"

Beckett smiled. "You already told me where she is."

"Okay." The bartender wilted. "I guess she's with Pelé Nascimento. I mean Santos Nascimento. We calls him 'Pelé' on account his name's the same as that Brazilian football player. Soccer to you, I guess. Santos was the best player San Vicente FC ever had, so we call him Pelé, too."

"Maybe he scores another way, too, Nevés? A joke? Pelé the big fix scorer? How come I don't know him?"

"He was away the two years you was with the sheriff."

"In jail?"

"I guess so. He been out three years, Mr. Beckett."

"That's a long time," Beckett said, paid for his beer.

Behind him as he left, men he hadn't even known were there moved out of the shadows toward the bar.

*

The owner of the *bodega* on Gutierrez Street grinned at Helen Sanchez as he packed the two bags of groceries.

"Where you get all the money middle of the week, Helen? Pelé rob a bank?"

"Pack the order, owner, shut your mouth," Helen Sanchez said. "You hear?"

The owner stopped grinning. "You got tight drawers?"

"Mind your business, owner. You could talk the wrong way to the wrong people, you know?"

The *bodega* owner licked his thin lips, packed the order without saying more.

Helen Sanchez picked up the bags. "Don't talk about me, owner. Okay?" she said.

"Sure, okay."

Helen Sanchez went out of the *bodega*, turned left, the small bell on the *bodega* screen door jangling behind her as the door closed. She walked east to Carson Street, turned south on Carson. She walked three blocks to a neat little house that needed paint but was almost hidden by flowers.

Inside the house, she put the bags on a kitchen table. A tiny old lady hobbled into the kitchen on a cane. Her black eyes snapped at Helen Sanchez from under tight-combed white hair like snow against her wrinkled brown skin.

"Did I ask for groceries, Helen? Why you bring?"

"They're not for you, Mama. I want you to keep them until Pelé comes to take them away."

"Pelé!" the old woman said. "I do not like that man. A bad Chicano, a bandit. A man who does not know his place is a man who will die in the prison."

"Don't say those things to me, Mama! You hear me?"

Helen said, faced the old woman. Then she shrugged. "He's better than I am, Mama, and they didn't make it easy for him."

The old woman stood her ground. "They? A man makes his own life, his own trouble. It is never easy, but if it is hard, it is a man's own fault."

"Maybe it is, Mama," Helen Sanchez said. "Just keep the groceries until Pelé comes to get them, okay?"

"What are you doing? You and that man?"

"Don't worry, Mama, it's all right."

"You tell me don't worry when I see more craziness? What do you do now? What badness?"

"It's all right, Mama."

"You are with those sick people again!"

"I have to go," Helen said. "Pelé will come soon. He will take the food, and leave. You don't know anything, you understand, Mama?"

"How could I not understand with you?"

Helen went back out into Carson Street, and walked three blocks to Salsipuedes Street. She turned north, and two blocks along Salsipuedes, opened the gate into a dirt yard littered with debris around a big, shabby gray house. A sign tacked to the porch read: *Rooms*. Helen looked into a box in the row of mailboxes, and went up to the second floor. She knocked three times on a door at the rear.

The man who opened the door was tall for a Mexican-American. Six feet and muscular, his thighs and calves bulging his tight trousers, he had a long face that owed as much to the conquistadors as to the Toltecs or Tlascalans. A face that had a yellow pallor against his dark, sunken eyes.

Helen kissed him. "The bags are at Mama's. Wait a little to be sure."

"We can't be sure," the man said. "It's no good."

"We do what we must, Pelé. Hey, where's my *hombre?*"

Pelé smiled. "You want *huevos,* too?" The smile faded. "We're fools, Helen. Crazy. They'll crucify us for it."

"What else could we do? No way, baby."

"Walk away! With our records? One slip, it's the end. All the work, the months. For what? If we're caught?"

"We won't get caught," Helen said.

Pelé laughed. There was no humor in the laugh. "The old story, eh? We won't get caught. How many times you said that before, Helen? The theme song—we won't get caught. Helen, we can't even trust anyone!"

"We have to. We'll make it."

"One more day, that's it. If it isn't over, we leave."

"We can't leave here, Pelé! Where would we go? Another year at least, unless we want to go back all the way."

"One day! Why the hell did we risk it, anyway?"

"Because we had to," Helen said.

In the silent room they looked at each other. Pelé turned and left without speaking again.

Alone, Helen Sanchez lighted a cigarette, and sat down. She smoked with her chin cupped in her hand.

*

Beckett crossed the littered yard to the big gray rooming house. He found the name of Helen Sanchez on the mailbox for 2-D. On the second floor, he knocked at 2-D.

"Hello, Helen," he said.

Small, with creamy brown skin, she might have been beautiful once, but her delicate face had both thickened and drawn tight in harsh lines. She looked no more than her thirty-plus years, but they had been long years.

"Mr. Beckett, right?" Helen Sanchez said.

"Three years, isn't it?" Beckett said. "How long did you get for that arrest?"

"Six months. Upstate. You got me into the country."

"I did you a favor. Can I come in?"

"You're asking now, Mr. Beckett?"

Beckett went into the room. A neat, clean room, with a double bed covered with a bright Mexican print. There were flowers on the bureaus and tables. An effort had been made to divide the single room into units: a bedroom unit with bed, dressing table, and night tables; a kitchen unit where another Mexican print covered a chipped enamel table; and a living room unit with a narrow couch, two armchairs, a battered coffee table, and a small TV set. Crowded, but not cluttered.

"I ask to come in because I'm not chasing you this time, Helen," Breckett said, faced her. "I'm after Roy Scott. All I want is help."

"You're back with the sheriff? I thought you didn't like him, Mr. Beckett?"

"I'm with Tucker, special investigator. Where's Roy?"

"How would I know, Mr. Beckett? A Scott with Chicanos?"

"He seems to like Chicanos. You were with him last night."

"We were with him, yes. A little while."

"You sold him pot, bennies, and what else?"

"We sold him nothing."

Beckett shook his head. "I know too much about you, Helen, and I called in about Pelé Nascimento. Smuggler, petty thief, dope peddler; fifteen arrests, five convictions, and not forty yet. He's spent half his life in jail, and so have you."

"Twenty-two arrests, fourteen convictions," Helen Sanchez said. "Misdemeanors: using, loitering, soliciting. I'll save you the trouble of looking me up."

"I don't have to look you up, Helen."

"We sold Roy nothing, we did nothing, Mr. Beckett."

"How about Stella Ortega? You sell her to him?"

"Stella knows him, too. He knew where to find her, and if he had marijuana or bennies, it wasn't from any of us."

"All right. Do you know where he is, Helen?"

"No."

Beckett watched her, and then he sat down. She didn't move from where she stood. A thin line of sweat beaded her brow at her dark hairline. Beckett leaned back.

"Ben Scott's a rich man," he said. "Easy to snatch a doped-up psycho already in a fog, and maybe scared. It might be easy to convince him he killed a man, offer to hide him, then make sure he stays hidden where you want him."

"We didn't see Roy since eleven-thirty last night!"

"A lot of drug money in Ben Scott's pockets," Beckett said. "This is a small city, Roy's pretty well known. A rich boy doesn't usually know how to hide in his own town. He moves in a small circle, a narrow world; doesn't know the hiding places."

"I don't know where he is, Mr. Beckett."

"Who was the man in the motel, Helen? The dead man?"

"I don't know. Roy looked us up, we knew him before. We had some drinks, talked in the motel."

"Just old times? He knew you three years ago, a rich kid slumming, playing with drugs. He was away three years, was back here six months, and never came near you. One day he needs marijuana, and he looks you up. Just for old times?"

"He wanted to talk. Something bad happened to him."

"What?"

"I don't know. He didn't make much sense."

"But he looked you up to talk nonsense?"

"Yes! He—"

Beckett was out of the chair, his hand on the pistol at his belt, as the door opened. He saw a tall Mexican man in the doorway. The look of an athlete gone heavy, yet not heavy enough—flabby, but wasted, too. Balanced on the balls of his feet like a bird about to fly away. A scared bird.

Helen Sanchez stepped toward the man. "Pelé, this is Mr. Beckett. He's working with the prosecutor's office, looking for Roy Scott. We're old friends, me and Mr. Beckett."

There was a struggle inside the tall man, but he closed the door, stood against it. His voice was low and thick. "Why look for Roy Scott here?" he said.

"He thinks we know where Roy is, that we sold him drugs," Helen Sanchez said. "I told him we have done nothing."

"I know both your records," Beckett said.

"A record is the past," Pelé said. "A record doesn't give you the right to threaten us without proof. You have proof?"

The ex-athlete's face was like one of the stone idols of his ancient people. The face that had at last resisted the conquistadors, hopeless but proud. The pride of a mild people who could be pushed too far, or the dignity of an athlete who remembered his own proud past.

Beckett said, "Don't be hard with me! You're scum, all of you. Addicts, pushers, joy-poppers. I hate you all. Ask Helen why someday, but now you remember I'll break you if you get wise with me!"

Pelé said, "I warn you, too! Don't lean your Anglocop weight on us until you have proof!"

They faced each other: Beckett broad and thick, in good shape; Pelé slimmer, younger, more muscular, but far out of shape. Pelé barely breathing; Beckett breathing too hard.

Helen Sanchez said, "Leave us alone, Mr. Beckett. We don't know anything we haven't said."

"You were with him," Beckett said. "A man was killed, and Roy's missing. Stella Ortega was the last one to see him. You're all up to your eyes in drugs. Maybe Stella hid him, and if she did, you two know it!"

"If Stella hid him, we don't know it."

Pelé said, "Ask Stella, not us!"

"I'm asking you," Beckett said. "You're all the same.

Like a nest of mice in the walls. You crawl all over each other, and what one does, the others know!"

He watched both with anger.

8

Stella Ortega had walked miles between the bare walls of her narrow room. All night and all day. Now, with another evening near, sweat beaded her parchment-like face. Four times in two hours she had gone to her one handbag. Each time it was as empty as the last time.

She had searched in every secret place where her cunning mind hid what she needed. There was nothing. She walked.

Sleep had come only fitfully since the police had finally let her go last night, and lying awake she had thought of Roy Scott. She had smiled, even in her desperation. He had come to her, and she remembered the hours in the motel, smiling.

She did not smile often through the night and day.

She paced the miles from wall to wall, smoked until her coffee-can ashtray overflowed onto the floor, and from time to time went to her one window that faced the slum street.

A cop was always out there watching her, waiting for her to lead them to Roy, or for Roy to come to her from wherever he had gone after Monday night. There was nowhere for her to go—they would follow.

If she lost them, the cops, there was still nowhere to go. She had to find somewhere, had to get what she needed. She could not last another night. But even if she lost them, the cops, they would find her. They knew everywhere she could go in San Vicente. There was no way for her, not in San Vicente.

She got her handbag, filled it with the few things she cared about, and went out the front door. She fought the pain of the afternoon sunlight against her eyes, and turned left, forcing herself to walk slowly. She did not look back.

She crossed three streets, and turned quickly into an alley. She ran ten steps, ducked through a loose board in a fence, ran into a house, and out into the next street. She ran across the street, along a path beside another house, and into another alley. There she waited ten minutes, biting her lip so hard it began to bleed. No one came after her.

Slowly she made her way through back alleys to the rear of the big gray rooming house where Helen and Pelé lived. She hurried up to apartment 2-D, pushed the door open: "Helen! I got to have money to get—"

She saw Beckett in the room. She screamed.

*

Stella Ortega sat on the bed, her thin shoulders like the sharp bones of a frightened bird.

"Money for who, Stella?" Beckett said. "You or Roy?"

"I don' see Roy since the night! I am with the police!"

"When did they let you go?

"Last night on'y! They take me home. I stay home."

"Maybe Roy was there already," Beckett said.

Helen Sanchez said, "You think they don't look, Mr. Beckett?"

"Roy had plenty of money," Pelé Nascimento said. "Stella wouldn't need money if Roy'd been with her."

Beckett said, "You can't run, Stella. You've got a short chain around your throat. For you, everywhere is the same. All we have to do is follow the chain, and pull."

Pelé said, "Leave her alone, Beckett."

"You took a fix that night, Monday, right?" Beckett said.

Stella shrank. "I take, *si.*"

"Okay, now tell me the real story of Monday night."

"I tell the cops a hundred times! I—"

"Who sent Roy to you, Stella? Helen and Pelé?"

"He come on his own. He found me at the Sportsman Bar." She shrugged. "I work there, you know?"

"What time?"

"A lil' after midnight."

Pelé said, "He left us around eleven-thirty."

Stella's face went distant. She sat on the bed as if she had been transported to some other level of her private hell. Her voice was soft. "He come to me. I see him, it is like the old days they come back. Roy, he like me 'cause I am so pretty." Her voice made it sound so long ago. She was perhaps twenty-one. "We have good times, a lil' while. Roy he is a Scott. I am girl sits at bars, already then I take the drugs. I have to live. I want the nice things ever'body else have, how I get them 'cept I hustle?"

A shadow crossed her thin face. "After a while I don' see Roy so much. He go to university, I don' get out of eighth grade. He's nice, but . . . Then he go in army." Her eyes blinked rapidly as if passing the last three years like some speeded-up movie of what she didn't want to remember. "I am ashamed he see me Monday. I am glad, but I am ashamed. I am not pretty, not young. Beat-up whore!"

Helen Sanchez said, "It ain't too late, Stell."

Stella said, "He kiss me, he act like he don' know I'm ugly. When he say we go to the motel, I go. In the motel it is nice. Before he go away he was a boy, too much the *hombre*. Now he is a man, slow and good. He make me feel almost pretty, almost like a girl."

She seemed to think about Monday night itself. "He is like he *sorry*. He act like he got to make it all okay for him before something happen. Like he know something got to happen, got to be how it is." There was a question in her eyes—how to say it?

"Fatalistic?" Beckett said. "Detached?"

"Like he know too much, got to hate what he knows. He play that record, say he don' know what is real. I . . . I got to have shot, so I go away. I hear noise like chair move inside. After I get my fix, I remember, and I am scared for him. I go back, he no answer. I get cops. A man is hang, but I do not know the man. I do not know what happen to Roy."

Helen Sanchez went to put her hand on the thin shoulder of the girl.

Beckett nodded. "Pretty story," he said, "but I'll tell you what really happened. Roy knew you because you sold him drugs in the past. He looked you up because he needed dope. Helen and Pelé sold him the marijuana and bennies, then steered him to Stella. He had money, you all planned to roll him, standard junkie operation. But something went wrong, and you killed that man at the Sierra. Was he a narcotics agent? Border patrol tracing the marijuana?

"Whatever, he caught you, and you killed him in a fight. Roy was drugged and half crazy. You got the idea to fake it to look like a psycho murder by hanging that dead man. You took Roy away. Maybe you killed him, too. He was suicidal, so we'll find him dead looking like a suicide. End of case. Close the books on a psycho murder and suicide. Only I'll dig it out, so you better run while you can. Run far and fast!"

"You will find nothing," Helen Sanchez said.

Pelé Nascimento said nothing. Stella shook on the bed.

*

An hour later Beckett stood hidden where he could see both the front and back way out of the rooming house. He had been there since leaving the room. No one had come out; no one he knew had gone in.

It was 3:00 P.M. when he went back inside, and up to apartment 2-D. He heard only silence inside. The door was locked. He opened the door with a small picklock. The room was empty.

Out in the corridor, he saw the open window at the far end. The roof of a side porch was under it. He swore softly, but there was no real anger in it. They had slipped him, but he went down to his car smiling.

The mice were running. They couldn't run far.

*

Sheriff John Hoag leaned against the wall in Prosecutor Charles Tucker's office.

"Nothing on the dead man?" Hoag said.

"No criminal record, nothing from Washington or Sacramento," Tucker said. "He wasn't any kind of cop, wasn't in the service, Missing Persons has no one who sounds like him. The clothes could have been bought in fifty stores. No cleaning tags or laundry marks."

"These home washing machines," Hoag said. "You're not far along, Charley. Maybe I better take the case back."

"Don't play games with me, John!"

"You can't identify the victim—and what has Beckett turned up? All he's done is chase the family. Where is he today?"

"I don't breathe down his neck."

"He worries me. What do we really know about him now?"

"I worry whose side you're on," Tucker said.

"The side of law, order and a square deal, Charley," Hoag said. "I was afraid I'd be biased in favor of the Scotts. Now I wonder if maybe you're biased against them to look like a crusading prosecutor."

"I'm just like you, John. All law and order."

"Then why are *you* playing games, Charley?"

"Am I?"

"You're digging into Ben Scott's business affairs."

"So your men are watching me and Beckett?"

"I watch what concerns me," Hoag said. "You're trying to mix Ben into Roy's actions. Some juicy scandal to build a reputation on, Charley? And I don't like Beckett digging up that arson thing on Roy Scott after I closed it."

"You think Ted Andrewski can't be part of what trouble Roy has now, John? You think Beckett's off-base with that, and with the drug angle?"

"I think he's fishing in empty water!"

Tucker leaned forward. "Then back off, John! Beckett found where Roy Scott was the last two weeks—a veterans' hospital near L.A., the mental section. Ted Andrewski was in the same hospital! Only Ted Andrewski was murdered early this morning—by someone who had to know the hospital."

"Andrewski? Killed?" Some of Hoag's blandness went.

Tucker nodded. "Beckett called it in. He's also found the other two who were with Roy on Monday night—a pair of known addicts with long records: Helen Sanchez and Pelé Nascimento. You could check out their actions instead of mine and Beckett's!"

"Lay off the speeches, Charley. What does Beckett say about Andrewski's murder? Roy?"

"The doctor at the hospital who treated both Roy and Andrewski thinks Roy could have done it. Beckett won't say yes or no yet. He says it's too early."

"Has anyone told the Scotts about Andrewski?"

"Beckett's on his way to the ranch now."

"All right," Hoag said. "It's getting too big. Maybe we *all* better find out who the hell that first dead guy was."

*

The Japanese houseman at the Charro Ranch told Beckett that none of the Scotts were at home. Beckett asked for the foreman Jess Rhine, and his daughter, and was directed to a small clapboard house under shade trees two miles farther along the dirt road. The main corrals and barns stretched all around the small house, and rows of bunkhouses were across a dusty square of ground.

An elderly woman answered Beckett's knock on the door of the small house. He asked for Janice or Jess Rhine.

"Janice isn't here, she's at work," the woman said. "Jess is over to the blacksmith shop. That's the shack over there just before the red barn."

"Are you Mrs. Rhine, ma'am?"

"No sirree! Mrs. Rhine been dead ten years now."

The sound of metal being hammered came from the blackened shack of the blacksmith shop. Inside, only one forge was being worked, its bed of coke glowing white-hot, small blue flames on its surface. The sour, pungent odor of hot metal filled the shack. A short, broad man held an incandescent bar in a pair of tongs, and a heavy hammer in his other hand.

"Mr. Rhine?" Beckett said.

"Yeh, I'm Jess Rhine."

Rhine was naked to the waist, his outdoor-working-man's body tanned heavily on face and forearms, pale everywhere else, and streaming sweat in black rivers over his muscles. His bull neck supported a flat face of solid features behind the thick mustache. Close to fifty, he had worked with his body all his life, and would look strong until one day he was an old man.

"My name's Lee Beckett," Beckett said. "Can I talk to you about your daughter and Roy Scott?"

Rhine laid the glowing metal rod on an anvil, and began to hammer in quick, light, shaping blows. "I heard about you. What can Janice tell you about Roy Scott? You found him yet?"

"No," Beckett said. "Janice was engaged to him."

"She's not now," Rhine said, studying his work closely as he hammered. "Looks like she'll marry Ham."

"What made her switch?"

"Good sense, and me," Jess Rhine said. He carried the metal rod back to the forge, pushed it into the coals, lit a cigarette. "Roy was gone three years, Beckett. That's a long time to a young girl. I told her which one was the better man, which one would get what Ben Scott's got."

"She wants what Ben Scott has?"

"I hope to hell she does," Rhine said. "Every fence post. Anyway, Ham suits her. They're good together. He needs her."

"What makes you sure Hamilton will take over for Ben, not Roy? You were sure even before this trouble?"

Rhine smoked, seemed to think it over. "Roy ain't the type for ranching or business. One of these new kind of kids. He always was. I don't try to figure what they want, only I know they don't want what me and Ben Scott went after. They got no use for everything that made life good for them. Okay, they can want what they want, but not my daughter. Janice and me talked the last three years. When Roy come home, she broke it off. Roy didn't even take it hard. No problem."

The foreman picked the rod from the coals with his tongs, began to hammer it again. He hit the anvil with rhythm blows as often as he hit the cherry-red rod.

"How did Janice take it?" Beckett said.

"She was low for a while, but she got over it."

"You're sure she got all over Roy, Rhine?"

The hammering rang through the shack.

"Why don't you catch Roy, Beckett?" Rhine said, hammered. "Or kill him. Do him a favor. Leave just Ham, make it easy."

"I'm trying. Where do I find Janice?"

Rhine went on working. "She works in town. Ben Scott's real estate office."

"Where Roy worked when he came home?"

"That's the place," Jess Rhine said. "Roy sat in that office while Ham learned the ranch. See?"

"You think the ranch is more important than the business?"

Jess Rhine was silent. Then he shrugged, hammered harder. "Maybe not, but I guess that don't matter much now."

*

Janice Rhine couldn't work. At her desk in the real estate office she looked at the empty desk where Roy Scott had sat only a few weeks ago. Where was he? Had he . . . killed that man? If not, what *had* he done?

She saw him in her mind, Roy, heard his voice again. Puppy love—for a crazy boy? And now—murder? She thought of Ham, and smiled. They wanted the same things, she and Ham. Only—did she really want what she seemed to want?

Her telephone rang. "Scott Management, Miss Rhine."

Silence.

"Hello? Scott Management, Miss Rhine speaking. Hello?"

Someone breathed at the other end of the line.

"Who is this?" Janice said.

The telephone made a loud noise as if it had hit against something at the other end. A woman's voice came on. "Hello?" the voice said. "Who is this, please?"

A woman with a faint Spanish accent.

"Janice Rhine at Scott Management. You called me."

"Sorry," the distant woman said. "A mistake."

The phone went silent. Janice stared at it. She was still holding it when the office boy came to her desk. "Soldier outside to see you, Jan," the boy said, and grinned. "A sergeant. I better tell Ham."

"A sergeant?" Janice hung up.

She walked quickly out to the reception room. A stocky man in a sergeant's uniform stood waiting. He was older than Roy, maybe thirty-five, but wore the same divisional patch. The service stripes on his uniform showed he was an old soldier.

"You're Janice?" the sergeant said. "I'm Anton Wicek from Roy's old outfit. I'm looking for Roy. His folks said he wasn't around when I called."

"No," Janice said.

"I'm passing through from L.A.," Wicek said. "I like to look up my boys. Roy used to talk about you."

"We . . . we broke up when he came home, Sergeant."

"That's too bad. Was he shook up? I mean, he was shook up some over there. That why you and him—"

"No, he was fine here. At least he was . . . I . . . I'm afraid Roy's in trouble, Sergeant Wicek. He's missing."

"Missing?" Wicek said. "Trouble?"

"Bad trouble," Janice said. "Poor Roy."

Wicek frowned. "Could we talk somewhere? I mean, maybe I can think of where he'd go, like that."

"Of course! I'll be right with you."

Janice ran back to tell the office manager that she had to go out. The manager wasn't pleased. Janice didn't care.

9

At Scott Management they told Beckett that Janice Rhine had gone out with a soldier.

"Some sergeant," the receptionist said.

"Where did they go?"

"I heard something about a bar."

Beckett hurried down to the street. He went through all the cocktail bars in the immediate downtown area. He found them in the Paloma Lounge. Janice Rhine waved to him.

"Mr. Beckett! Do you have any—?"

"No." Beckett nodded to the sergeant. "Who's this?"

"Anton Wicek," the sergeant said, shook hands. "I knew Roy over in Nam, Mr. Beckett."

Janice said, "He doesn't know where Roy could be."

Beckett heard the sharp disappointment in her voice. She wanted to find Roy Scott very much. Why? Ham's girl? Beckett filed it in his mind, but spoke to Anton Wicek.

"What are you doing in San Vicente, Sergeant?"

"On my way from L.A. to Frisco. I'll be going back to Nam. I like to look up my old boys."

"What can you tell us about Roy?"

"He was one good soldier, I'll tell you that," Wicek said. "The new kind, not much for orders and always asking why, but quiet and did his job—until he cracked up."

"Battle fatigue?"

"I guess. It's a hard war to take, a lot crack. Roy went back to Saigon for some months. I heard they had to send him to the shrinks, but he seemed okay last I saw him."

"When was that?"

"In Japan, about a week before he came home."

"Did he get into any trouble besides the war itself? Something he might have done?"

"Not that I heard. 'Course, I was in the jungle when he was back in Saigon the last months."

Beckett turned to Janice. "Did Roy ever mention anything wrong in his letters?"

"No. He didn't write many—" She looked at the floor. "So you found out."

"Why didn't you say you'd been Roy's fiancée?"

"I don't know," she said. "I mean, I *really* don't know. I guess I just didn't want to talk about it. No reason."

"You fell in love with Ham while Roy was away?"

"Yes, I guess so."

"Don't you know, Janice?"

"Yes, I know," she said. "I grew up while Roy was gone. Ham and I saw a lot of each other with Roy away, we found we think alike, I guess. When Roy came home, I was sure. He was so much older. So I broke it off. He seemed almost glad. That made me mad at first, but I guess it was only puppy love."

"Doubts?" Beckett said.

"No, I love Ham. Only . . . Roy's out there all alone."

Sergeant Wicek said, "We come home, and no one wants us. Don't bother us, soldier. We're fools or killers!"

"Do you know Ted Andrewski, too, Sergeant?" Beckett asked.

"Sure," Wicek said. "I heard about his trouble. He's not like Roy. A good soldier, but only when you told him what to do. I guess when he got home, he flipped—not knowing how to take the ways people act about Vietnam, no one to tell him what to do."

"You looked him up, too?"

"I don't even know where Ted is now."

"He's dead, Sergeant, that's where he is." Beckett told them about the hospital. "Roy knows that hospital."

Wicek looked sick. "No! Him and Roy got along. Christ, Ted went through a year getting shot at, and not a bruise."

Janice Rhine said, "They think that maybe Roy—?"

"We don't know yet. We have to find him."

"Don't you have any ideas where he'd be?" Wicek said.

Janice said, "Mr. Beckett? I had a funny telephone call a little while ago," and she described the silent call, and the woman's voice that had come on the line.

"A Spanish accent, you're sure?" Beckett said.

"Yes. Not much of an accent. You . . . you think it could have been Roy? That silence at first, I mean?"

"Maybe he's tired of running, needs to talk to someone. I've seen that before with fugitives, the silence and fear gets to a man," Beckett said. He stood up.

Sergeant Wicek said, "Okay if I hang around a few days? I'm at the Flamingo Hotel. I mean, maybe I could help take Roy without hurting him."

"Okay, stay around," Beckett said as he walked out.

*

No one had returned to room 2-D in the gray rooming house where Helen Sanchez and Pelé Nascimento lived. Beckett drove on to Stella Ortega's room on San Rafael Street. It was at the rear of a dilapidated stucco house, with a private side door. Beckett didn't see Stella's Mustang, or the old blue Ford. There was no sound inside the room, and the door was locked. Beckett used his picklock again.

As he closed the door, he saw all the pulled-out bureau drawers and heard the sound behind him in the room.

"Just stand," a steady voice said. "I've got a pistol."

There was a cracking sound like a whip. Plaster broke from the wall Beckett was facing, and left a small hole. A silenced pistol.

"So you don't have to turn to be sure."

Beckett didn't turn. A hand patted him for weapons, removed his gun from his belt holster.

"Sit down."

Beckett sat. The man came around to where Beckett could see him. It was the slender, thin-faced, almost delicate young man he had seen on the beach below the Sierra

93

Motel. The man held a long-barreled pistol and wore the same good dark gray suit. His white shirt and dark blue tie looked as expensive as the suit, and his posture was straight and firm. Neither his small mouth nor his cool eyes had even the trace of a smile. A hard, serious, confident face. Beckett guessed that the man wasn't thirty yet.

"You caught me in here, so now we'll talk. I'm looking for Roy Scott, Mr. Beckett."

"What else are you looking for?"

"Roy is enough," the young man said, balanced lightly on the balls of his small feet, in full control. "I think we can work out something."

"Why do you want Roy Scott?"

"That doesn't matter to anyone but me."

"It does to this county. We want him here."

"Maybe you can have him later, or maybe it won't matter," the young man said. "I'll pay you twenty-five thousand dollars to deliver him to me if you find him. You'll keep quiet about it, and let me try to find him, too. A deal?"

Beckett appeared to think. "You knew Roy in the army, right? In Vietnam? Officer's written all over you. A lieutenant, from your age. Combat?"

"Enough, and it was captain. The deal?"

"What do you do with him if you get him?"

"That depends on what he says. It's a fair price, Beckett."

"Kill him?"

"What do you care? He's a murderer, isn't he? Twice over. Maybe he's insane, he's certainly irrational. You'll kill him if he resists."

"We'll take him alive if we can. I'd have to know

more about why you want him. I'd need that to know what to tell to cover my actions."

"You'll think of a story. Maybe we won't even hurt him. Then you'd have the money, and I'd turn him over as well."

Beckett thought again. "You know a Sergeant Anton Wicek, too?"

"Wicek? Why?"

"He's here looking for Roy. An old friend, he says."

The slender man frowned. "I know him. I don't like it much, Beckett, but the deal stands. Well?"

Beckett shrugged. "It's not so much money."

"Try thirty-five thousand dollars then."

"You want him a lot, or you've got a lot of money lying around loose," Beckett said. "Maybe for fifty thousand, I might—"

The man waved the pistol. "Don't bargain with—"

The pistol pointed away for an instant. Beckett jumped. His powerful leg muscles charged him against the slender man. He had the man's gun wrist, bent the pistol away. The thin young man was strong, his arms like steel springs, but he was no match for Beckett's size and weight. He made no sound, only fought in Beckett's grip with his cold eyes on the big investigator's face.

Beckett bulled him against a wall, hit him with a short, solid left in the jaw. The man's head snapped back, cracked against the wall. When the head bounced forward, Beckett hit the jaw again. The man went limp. Beckett caught him and lowered him to the floor.

Beckett laid the man's pistol on a bare table, found his own gun and holstered it. He searched the man. There was money, keys, and a wallet. The wallet contained five hundred dollars and a ten-thousand-dollar draft on an L.A. bank in the name of the Camvin Company. It also held papers identifying the slender young man as Captain Peter Mark, Military Police, U.S. Army, and a plastic photostat of discharge papers less than six months old.

Beckett sat down. He looked at the unconscious man, who was beginning to move. The man still made no sound. Captain Peter Mark, who was, or had been, an M.P. officer. After Roy Scott—undercover? Why? Somehow, the offer of a bribe didn't sound very official. Roy had been in Vietnam only a few—

The window broke to Beckett's left. The muzzle of a forty-five automatic poked through the broken pane straight at Beckett. His own pistol was on his belt. He sat motionless. The forty-five continued to point at him—and nothing else. A gun, a vague hand, and a silence that seemed to stretch on and on.

Behind Beckett, Captain Peter Mark moved. The slender man seemed to be on his feet. The outer door opened and closed. The forty-five still rested on the window sill. A car door opened somewhere outside. The forty-five vanished. Beckett jumped up. Captain Mark was gone—with his gun. Beckett went to the outer door carefully. Something held it closed from the outside. Beckett went to the windows, unlocked the broken one, and climbed out.

There was no car on the street, no one in sight.

Beckett went back to the door of Stella Ortega's room. The knob had been tied to a nail in the frame by a length of plastic cord. Beckett untied the cord. He searched Stella's room. He found nothing at all.

*

Charles Tucker said, "An M.P. captain? What does he want?"

"He didn't tell me," Beckett said. He smoked in the chair across the desk from the prosecutor. "He thinks Roy killed our victim and Andrewski. I wonder if that means he knows who the dead man is, too?"

"If he does, he's ahead of us. Either the dead guy covered himself all the way like an expert, or he's so ordinary there's almost nothing to find out about him. You'd think that someone would have missed him by now, reported him."

"You would," Beckett agreed. "Better check Captain Peter Mark out with Washington. Find out who he is, what he did in the army. And ask about the Camvin Company, too."

"Okay," Tucker said, "and I've got something for you. I dug into Ben Scott's business affairs. I—"

"You think Ben Scott's business is part of this?"

"I like to work all possible angles."

"Nice," Beckett said. "You don't plan to be a county prosecutor all your life, do you, Charley? You could use some nice headline-type dirt."

"Ambition bothers you, Lee?"

"That depends on what it makes a man do. What it leads to."

"Maybe it leads to a motive," Tucker said. "Around three weeks ago, just before Roy Scott vanished, Ben Scott raised some hell about land reports. No details yet, but there was talk of fraud. He had a private session with his office manager, and the manager worked late a lot of nights. No word on what the fraud could be, but Ben's got a big land deal in the works with a New York-based oil company."

Beckett stubbed out his cigarette. "Find me who our first dead man was, Charley, and keep after Captain Peter Mark."

Alone in the office, Charles Tucker looked at the view of the sea from his windows. A twilight haze obscured the distance, but Tucker watched the view for some time anyway. Then he picked up his phone.

"Wes? Keep after Ben Scott's business, harder. And check into the wife, too. Anything you can find."

*

In the rear sitting room of the ranch house, Marlene Scott, wearing a brief tennis dress, smiled over her gin-and-tonic at the tall, handsome man.

"Ben went off early this morning, Martin. Does it matter where?"

"It depends on just where, and why," Martin Elder said.

Over six feet, Elder was trim and well built for a man of fifty. Not broad, but not thin, his dark hair was gray at the temples, with every strand in place as if a barber traveled with him. He wore tennis clothes like a man born to casual elegance.

"Up to Monteverde, Jess Rhine says," Marlene said. "Are you worried about the oil land? I guarantee the deal."

"It's not a major project, but I have the reputation of successfully completing every job I handle. That reputation is important. Can you guarantee the deal, Marlene?"

"You're saying my influence over Ben has slipped?"

"I've noticed some change this time. He's moody. He's acting rustic, restless with your New York style. Is he?"

"He's got a lot on his mind."

"Us, Marlene?"

"That, too, perhaps," she said. "What is our New York style, Martin?"

"The best of everything all the time. Cultivate the world as it is, use it for our pleasure and comfort and power."

"Is that my style, Martin? And yours?"

Elder smiled. "Some people were born to it, a simple fact. In a democracy, someone must operate the machinery ordinary people think operates by itself. Someone has to manipulate the process to keep the machinery running the same. We have to make sure the people choose the right men at the right time to do the right things."

"How do we do that?"

"By making sure that they choose the man we want. Make the choice they have between A, B and C result in our getting the man for us as often as we can, if not always."

"By seeing to it that A, B and C are *all* our men, yes?"

Elder walked to her. "You, woman, are too smart."

She put her arms around his neck and kissed him.

10

When Lee Beckett walked into the ranch living room in the early evening twilight, Marlene Scott was sitting on a couch in a white tennis dress. A tall man in tennis shorts stood over her. Marlene saw Beckett's face, and sat up alarmed.

"Mr. Beckett? Roy's not—?"

"We haven't found him," Beckett said. He told her about Ted Andrewski and Dr. Emil Remak.

"A mental hospital? Roy? That's ridiculous!"

"He didn't think so, he went voluntarily," Beckett said. "You're not concerned about Ted Andrewski?"

"Do you know that Roy . . . killed him?"

"No."

"Then why should I care about a man who's been nothing but trouble to Roy? Dead or alive?"

"He may be a lot more trouble dead, Mrs. Scott."

She stood, slim and angry. "Has anyone even seen Roy? Have you any proof of anything except that he's hiding, afraid? If he committed himself to a mental hospital, doesn't that explain his fear? Perhaps if you stopped hounding after him, he'd come home by himself!" She took a breath, looked at the tall man. "I'm sorry, Martin. This is Mr. Beckett of the county prosecutor's staff. He's looking for my son Roy, who may be in trouble. Mr. Beckett, Martin Elder from New York."

"Beckett," Martin Elder said. He didn't offer his hand, as if Beckett's status and income bracket didn't require it.

"Elder," Beckett said. "You're buying land from Ben Scott?"

Marlene Scott said, "Martin is executive vice-president of Rio Oro Petroleum. My husband has some promising land."

"Any problems about the land?" Beckett asked.

Elder said, "Do you know of any?"

Beckett didn't answer. "Is your husband home, Mrs. Scott?"

"He drove somewhere this morning. Monteverde, I think."

"This morning? How early?"

"He was gone when I got up at eight-thirty. Why?"

"What do you know about some kind of fraud in your husband's real estate office?" Beckett said.

"Fraud? Nothing at all."

"About the time Roy went away," Beckett said.

Martin Elder said, "What kind of fraud? Land?"

"We don't know yet," Beckett said.

Marlene Scott said, "You think Roy could have been

part of some fraud against Ben? Who could be feeding you such drivel? Ben dotes on Roy! They never had any trouble!"

"Does Roy dote on Ben, Mrs. Scott?"

Marlene Scott started to speak, and stopped.

"Dr. Remak says Roy acted as if he hated Ben, and you," Beckett said bluntly.

"Did he now? Just who is this Remak?"

"He treated Roy in Japan. Roy never talked about him?"

"If he had, I wouldn't ask you," Marlene snapped. She was silent a moment. "Roy was difficult as a boy, then— what do you say?—too big for his breeches later. Too sure we were wrong. I never met his friends at the university, but I know them—radical fools and windy failures!"

"Roy was against you and Mr. Scott? Even when he came home?"

"At one time or another he opposed us in everything. Not as much recently, though. I'd have said he was closer to us than he'd ever been. If he said he hated us, I don't know why."

"Maybe he doesn't know himself," Beckett said. "Does your first husband have anything against you or Roy?"

"Howard? Why should he? I was seventeen when I married him, and I left him when I realized he would never give me what I needed. I wasn't made for a plebian life, happy for a roof, babies, and food. I think Howard was glad to be shut of me."

"And glad to lose his son?"

"No, I think that hurt him. Life isn't always simple."

"He seems bitter. Angry at the name Scott."

She shrugged. "He might have hoped for Ben's help. A good job, perhaps. That didn't appeal to me as an idea. I lost all interest in Howard Sill twenty-two years ago."

"Maybe he didn't lose all interest in you," Beckett said.

Before Marlene could answer, the telephone rang, and the Japanese houseman appeared in the room almost at once.

"It is Mr. Ben, Mrs. Scott," the Japanese said.

Marlene stood up. "I'll tell him you want to talk to him, Mr. Beckett."

She left the two men alone with each other.

*

Marlene picked up the receiver. "Ben? Where—?"

The voice was low, tight, "Hello, Mother."

"Who . . ." Marlene began, and, "Roy? Roy, where are—?"

Roy Scott laughed at the other end. "Hiding. Running and hiding, the bloodhounds of the great society after me. They're efficient bloodhounds, I'm feeling tired, but . . . You remember when Ben and I used to fish the river when I was a kid? The shack? Come alone, Mother, I'm too tired to run much more."

"The shack? You want me to . . . Roy, please, come home and give—"

"Don't tell me to give myself up, Mother. The problem is settled, after a slight delay. I just want to talk to you."

"Roy, dear, you're confused, and—"

"Irrational. A psycho. I know. I suddenly want to talk to my mother. That's irrational enough, isn't it? I'll wait an hour or so. Just you, no one else. A reunion."

At the far end of the line he laughed, and hung up. Marlene held the receiver for some time before she put it down.

*

Martin Elder smoked in the living room. "Have you been a policeman long, Mr. Beckett?"

"Twenty-five years, off and on."

"That long? Is it interesting work?"

"Yes, but it doesn't pay or get me much status."

"A man is worth his hire," Elder said.

"Everyone has his way of getting through a short life," Beckett said. "Some grab for all they can as fast as they can, act as if it all goes on forever. Others see the shortness, try to be part of a human stream that goes on by working to make life better for everyone. In the end it doesn't matter if you helped or hurt, got rich or changed society. At the end I suspect it all seems like the blink of an eye, both good times and good works unimportant, hard to even remember."

"You're a cynic, Mr. Beckett."

"You're a cynic, Elder, I'm a nihilist. I don't think either J. P. Morgan or Gandhi died happy or even content."

"You didn't develop that observation out here."

"In New York, the same as you. I watched people. Only people commit horrors. Being human consists of the acts we call inhuman. Until we see that, we'll get nowhere. But my theory is based on what happened to me, it's probably as wrong as any other theory."

"Nothing true? You frighten me. Is that what you want—?"

Marlene Scott came back. She sat down and lit a ciga-

104

rette without waiting for Martin Elder's proffered lighter. "Ben's manager, not Ben," she said to Beckett. "About our party on Sunday. You must come."

"If I can, thanks."

"I . . . I feel I haven't been any help. Is there any—?"

"You said Roy never talked about specific trouble he might have had. Did he mention a Captain Peter Mark? Or a Sergeant Anton Wicek?"

"The captain, no. Not the sergeant, either, but a Sergeant Wicek called here today. An old friend of Roy's, he said. I told him Roy wasn't here."

"Tell me if he calls again, and tell your husband I want to talk to him when he gets back."

"Yes," Marlene said. "Of course."

*

At the window, Marlene Scott watched the dust cloud of Beckett's car going away. She turned to Martin Elder. "I have to leave, Martin. I'll see you later at the hotel."

"I'll be in the bar at nine."

"No, in your room. It's better for now."

She kissed the tall executive again, and went out of the house to her small open Jaguar. She put on a pair of dark glasses and drove off down the dirt road.

On the highway, she drove to the fork that led south into the rough country. When she reached the old settlement of Silver Camp, the sun was low behind the Santa Ysolde Mountains to the west. She turned into a dirt road that wound west beside the Santa Ysolde River into the foothills. Dry now in the shadows of the trees, the river was deep and rushing in the winter rains when the up-stream dams spilled.

She pulled off the dirt road in front of a cabin at the edge of a pool in the river that still had some water even in the dry season. She smoked a cigarette, watched the cabin. A blue Chevy Nova was parked behind the cabin. No one came out. She got out of the car, ground her cigarette out under her foot in the reflex action of people who live in dry country, and went into the cabin.

She closed the door behind her.

"Greetings," Roy Scott said.

given us!" The pistol cut the dark air of the cabin like the sword of an Eastern fanatic. "Christ, that's horrible. It should make us gentle, selfless, aware of our fragility and enjoying each minute. Why live if it doesn't? Nothing can last except the minutes themselves."

Marlene smoked, her marble face busy. Thinking, not listening to what she had heard before, did not care about. "Martin wasn't here when you left," she said. "You couldn't have known about Martin then."

"I've had time to watch and think the last couple of days. Nothing else to do—watch and think," Roy said.

"It wasn't why you left," Marlene said. "It's not why all of . . . this. That Dr. Remak at the hospital you went to, he says you hate us, Ben and me. Why? Why did you leave?"

"Remak? The bloodhounds are even more efficient," Roy said. "Why? Because of what you did, Mother. You and Ben. What you did, and what you can't help doing."

"Did? To you? We did nothing to you!"

"Don't think, Mother. It can't help."

"You need help, Roy. Please? The police are hunting you like an animal! You'll be hurt, perhaps . . . killed. Roy, let me call the police. You called me, you want help. You—"

"A good son talks to his mother, doesn't he?" Roy said. "No police, Mother. I'll go in my own time. Soon now."

"Don't talk like that!"

"All right, I won't talk about it. But it's not something bad. I learned that in Vietnam, too. Why go on paying for space I can't use?"

Marlene dropped her cigarette to the cabin floor. "Did you kill that man at the motel, Roy? Did you kill Ted Andrewski today?"

"It doesn't—" The pistol wavered in his hand. "Ted? Did I kill Ted? Today?"

"At that hospital. Why didn't you say you felt sick?"

Roy shook his head as if to clear away a fog before his eyes. "Ted? Killed? No, I . . . I don't think . . ." His eyes squeezed together as if trying to see the last few days somewhere inside his mind.

"They can't blame you, dear. Ben will talk to Hoag."

His eyes opened, watched her face. "You think I killed them? Do you like to think that your sons have the ability to kill if they have to? If it's important?"

His body went limp, loose. He stood up at the table, the pistol aimed at Marlene. She made a sound. Only a sound, nameless.

"Ted shouldn't be dead," he said. "Not Ted, no. We'll finish it, Mother. Let Ben Scott and Martin Elder have their illusions. That's better. You'll only grow old."

"Roy!" There was panic in her eyes. "We all want to help you! Hamilton, Ben, Janice. Everyone wants to help!"

He scowled. "Everyone wants, yes. That's one more thing I learned in Nam. Everyone wants, so let them have. Help them have, why not? No right or wrong. You don't want to grow old, Mother, do you?"

"Roy—!"

Her panicked eyes saw Beckett before Roy did. The big man was silently through the rear door, in the dark room. Roy heard and turned. Beckett was five feet away from the youth. Roy's gun was leveled. Beckett dove at him.

Roy jumped aside.

Beckett sprawled on the floor.

He came up half-crouched, the pistol in Roy Scott's hand aimed at his eyes.

Ten seconds passed.

Roy Scott made no move.

Beckett stood up, stepped to the youth, took the pistol, put it in his pocket. He handcuffed Roy Scott's hands, sat him down again in the chair. Roy looked at the far wall.

Marlene Scott sat, sweat beading her beautiful face.

Beckett said, "You're a fool, Mrs. Scott."

She was shaking. "He's my son. You followed me?"

"That phone call was too simple. I saw something wrong."

"Yes, of course. What happens now?"

"I take him in. Go home and find your husband. Tell him to get his lawyer to the jail."

"Yes, all right," Marlene said.

Beckett said, "Roy? Come on."

Roy Scott stood up. He had said nothing since Beckett came into the cabin, he said nothing now. Beckett put him into the official car, re-handcuffed him to the front-seat armrest in the seat next to the driver. Then Beckett got in, and the car drove away.

Marlene Scott stood in the dusk at the cabin door. She watched Beckett drive away. Then she went back into the cabin. She found the telephone in an empty inner room. It was working, Roy had called her on it. She picked it up, dialed.

"Sheriff Hoag, please."

She waited.

"John? Beckett's got Roy, yes. He's sick, John, Roy is. He even threatened me. Yes. I'm afraid of Beckett, John. You understand me? I want Roy safe."

*

Beckett drove, said, "Did you kill that man in the Sierra, Roy?"

The blond youth's face was turned away toward the car window, and the rough country that passed outside in the dusk. His left hand jerked from time to time like the hand of a puppet on some invisible string.

"I killed a woman once. Under a train. I wonder who she really was?" The back of his blond head moved from side to side as Beckett watched him. "I was on the subway platform. She was standing at the edge. The train came in, and I pushed her under it. She was just there on the platform in New York."

His head turned to face front. His eyes were like those of a sleepy infant who looked out at the amazing world but had no idea of what it saw. "I've never been in New York, but I knew that subway platform was in New York. I decided to kill the woman when I saw her there. I saw her a lot at the end in Nam. I pushed her, and the train went right over her. I just walked away. Simple. She screamed, but no one noticed, of course. I still wonder who she was."

"Who was that man at the Sierra, Roy?" Beckett said.

Roy leaned his head back against the car seat, looked up at the roof, his eyes wide and white. "Who knows?"

"We'll find out, Roy."

"Find out? Find out what?" His eyes rolled all white at the roof of the car.

"Who the dead man in your motel room was."

"Dead man? What dead man?"

"The man we found hanging instead of you," Beckett said. "By your rope. You intended that rope for yourself, or did you? Was it all an act? A crazy attempt to cover murder?"

Roy Scott closed his eyes. "Over there I got interested in Buddha. Peace that passeth understanding. I read about that peace. Between kills."

The car had reached the fork where the county road joined the highway, and Beckett turned toward the Santa Ysolde Mountains as the highway began to climb. Roy Scott didn't open his eyes or move.

"Walk in the sun—at peace," Roy said. "A simple ball of fire, a physical accident, no meaning. All of life, the sun, because it made us. Heat created us. No meaning. So sit in the sun and try to be at peace with yourself."

He opened his eyes, lowered his head, stared ahead in the last light of dusk at the road and the mountains all around. "You can't be at peace, not in this country. No chance. Sit and think, and you're a bum. You'll starve, if they don't stone you to death. It has to be honored before it can be done."

He fell silent as the car wound upward around the sharp curves toward the summit of Silver Camp Pass. Almost dark now, Beckett driving carefully with his lights on.

Beckett said, "I don't think you killed that man. I

don't think you knew who he was, and maybe you still don't know. Who did kill him, Roy? Why?"

"You don't think I killed him? What are you, man, some kind of nut?" Roy said, and laughed aloud.

"No, and I don't think you're crazy, either," Beckett said. "I think you were depressed, irrational, suicidal. Not crazy, no. I think you knew what you were doing. But something happened that made you run away instead. Something that's made you wonder for over two days if suicide is the answer."

Roy Scott laughed again, loud. "Oh, man, I'm crazy enough! Believe me. Not as much as everyone else, maybe, but enough. Not as insane as the world, but not sane, nossir."

"You bought the rope, the pot, and the bennies. You took Stella Ortega to the room. You sent her away, rigged the rope, played your record—and then what happened, Roy?"

They were near the top of the pass, with the night fully dark.

Roy Scott looked down toward the lights of San Vicente. "When we were up near Da Nang we had a hell of a good body count one day," he said. "It looked good on the scoreboard, and we had a beautiful string of bodies for the camera. We—"

"Did Helen and Pelé kill that man, Roy? They sold you the pot and bennies, and the man came after them?"

Roy's eyes seemed to clear, become almost normal. His left hand jerked again, but his voice was steady. "Leave them out of it," he said.

"They're in it."

"No. They sold me nothing, did nothing. We talked,

no more. They tried to talk me into dancing to the tune. Later they helped me when I ran to them. They're friends. Leave them alone, you know?"

"If they hid you they're in trouble. Tell me what happened at the motel after four A.M. that night."

"Nothing," Roy said. "I don't remember. I'm crazy —ask Dr. Remak. I'm a nut, I don't know real from dream."

"Crazy enough to drive down and kill Ted Andrewski?"

"How do I know? Maybe I did. Why not? I guess I did. Who else would want to kill Ted?"

"Why would you want to kill him?"

"Who knows? Maybe I told him—"

They were going down the pass in long curves, the mountains to the left, the steep drops to the right.

"Told him what, Roy?" Beckett said.

"My crazy dreams. Maybe I told him my nutty dreams. You have to kill a man to get your dreams back."

"Why is Captain Peter Mark after you?"

The blond youth's face underwent a slow change. He turned toward Beckett in the car as if in slow motion. His face had become blank and smooth like polished stone. "Captain Mark?" he said. "After me? Here?"

"Here and now. He wants you a lot."

"Mark?" Roy blinked. "Can I have a cigarette?"

His voice was normal again. Beckett gave him a cigarette, lit it. Roy smoked and looked ahead to where the highway leveled on the lower slopes of the mountains as it came into San Vicente. Two cars were coming up toward Beckett's car, their headlights close together.

"Poor Ted," Roy said. "He made it in Nam up to the

last month. The last month broke him. Waiting for the tour to end, counting the days and hours, afraid to step out of the bunker even to the latrine. Why would Pete Mark kill Ted?"

"You think Mark killed him? What does Mark want, Roy?"

"Everything. Pete Mark wants it all. But why—?"

Beckett saw the two cars ahead. Sheriff's cars across the highway to block it, their red lights flashing, men around them. One deputy stood out on the road. He waved Beckett to a stop. Beckett hit his brakes, slowed . . .

The windshield shattered between him and Roy. Something snapped through the car, smashed a rear side window. Two shots, like the cracking of a giant whip, reverberated from the slopes.

Beckett ducked by reflex, lost control. The car skidded, slewed back, almost went over, and left the road. It plunged down the last gentle slope of the pass, sideswiped two trees, slowed more, swung sideways, and smashed the left rear into a third tree.

*

Beckett opened his eyes. His head pounded, his left shoulder was on fire, his knee stabbed pain. He reached for the car door.

The door wasn't there. Nothing was there.

He was on the ground twenty feet from the car, which had begun to burn. No one was near him. Far off, people were running. Who had pulled him out? Roy . . . ?

He raised himself up. The car was empty.

Beckett fell back, the pain sweeping a black wave over him.

Feet ran up.

The face of Sheriff John Hoag looked down at Beckett.

12

They stitched a gash in Beckett's head in the hospital, reduced and strapped his dislocated shoulder, X-rayed his swollen left knee, found no internal injuries, and sedated him.

He slept without thinking about Roy Scott.

He awoke in the morning, and thought about Roy Scott.

He got out of bed, and fell flat as his knee gave way. They got him back into bed. When Charles Tucker arrived at the hospital, Beckett raised up in bed.

"Roy got away?"

Tucker nodded. "No trace. He got the handcuff key from your pocket. He dragged you out before he ran, Lee."

"Yeh," Beckett said.

"We found two thirty-thirty rifle shells a hundred

yards up on a fire road. We'll need the rifle to match the shells."

"What was Hoag doing out there?"

"Marlene Scott called from the cabin. She told Hoag you had Roy. He went out to take charge. He probably saved your life, Lee. The roadblock made you slow down when whoever it was on the mountain fired."

"I should have known she'd whistle for Hoag," Beckett said. "No clue to who shot at us?"

"No, and no leads to where Roy Scott is now."

"He knows Captain Mark, Charley. Any news on Mark?"

"I'm still waiting on Washington," Tucker said. "Roy had a blue Chevy Nova at that cabin. No registration, but I'll bet it's the car of our dead man. I'm checking it out."

"Okay, and get Sergeant Wicek here. He's at the Flamingo Hotel. I want him."

Tucker said, "Hoag's talking about taking the case back. He says you were careless, and you're out of action. Marlene Scott says you went off half-cocked to intimidate Roy."

"Building a defense before a charge is made," Beckett said. "Maybe it doesn't matter. I think that sniper was after Roy, not me. Someone wants Roy dead."

*

By the second morning Beckett was hobbling around the room.

The doctor said, "You were badly injured once, right? Leave too soon, you could be a cripple for life."

Beckett went back to bed. He had a horror of being crippled. Tucker came again in the afternoon.

"We've got him, Lee! Our dead man. The car was his," Tucker said. "Edward Radin of Monteverde, a county local. Aged thirty-two, expert on land titles and mineral rights. A hundred-percent clean. No record, no military service."

"Land titles and rights?" Beckett said. "Ben Scott?"

"That's it," Tucker said. "Radin worked in the Monteverde office of Scott Real Estate Management. I haven't told anyone, I figured you'd want to do that yourself. Radin's sister is coming down to make the official ident."

Beckett nodded slowly. "What about Captain Peter Mark, and where's Sergeant Wicek?"

"I've got the report from Washington, but Wicek's gone, Lee. He checked out of the Flamingo early this morning."

"Yeh," Beckett said. "What's the word on Captain Mark?"

Tucker drew a form from his inside pocket. "Captain Peter S. Mark, age twenty-six. Born, Cleveland, Ohio; present residence, Cleveland. West Point, Class of 1965. Military Police. One year San Francisco Presidio. One year Adjutant-General's Office, Washington, D.C. Three years Vietnam. Returned to U.S., resigned commission December, 1970. Entered Cleveland electronic firm as partner, ran for local office, lost."

"He bought into an electronics company right out of the army? A partner?" Beckett said.

"The report doesn't say how he got into the business."

"No," Beckett said.

*

On Saturday Beckett tested his knee. It held. His shoulder hurt, but not too much, and by 10:00 A.M. he was in Tucker's office as the prosecutor brought in a heavy young woman.

"Miss Radin, this is Mr. Beckett," Tucker said. "Tell him about your brother."

"That's Eddie in the morgue," she said. She sat heavily in a chair. "I hadn't seen him for maybe two weeks, only he called last Monday, said the job was going to take longer, so I didn't think anything, you know? Poor Eddie." She looked up at them both. "Why, you know? I mean, what was Eddie that anyone would kill him? A desk jockey—nine-to-five, half-hour lunch, a movie on Saturday."

Beckett said, "Did he use drugs, Miss Radin?"

"You mean dope? Eddie? God, no! A beer twice a week," she said. "Maybe he should have, you know? Done something. Not Eddie. Honest and sober. Never took a dime he didn't do fifteen cents' work for. I told him. Eddie, I said, you going to work all your life making money for other people? The company was God. Look what it got him." '

"Was he ever in the Orient?" Beckett asked.

"He never left the state except to go to Canada once. Just over the border, Vancouver! Who killed him, Mr. Tucker?"

"We don't know yet."

She nodded, looked down at her hands. "Not that it matters. Dead's dead. He had some insurance. I suppose I get it, he never married. He never did anything. If he had any fun, he didn't tell me about it."

"What job was he doing in San Vicente?" Beckett said.

"Something for his boss. Scott Management, the whole story of Eddie's life. Paperwork. He started in the field, a surveyor, but he couldn't handle people. He was a whiz at the paperwork."

"When did he come to San Vicente?"

"Today's Saturday? Well, like I said, about two weeks ago, Monday before last."

"And you talked to him on the phone last Monday?"

"That's right, around nine P.M. it was."

Beckett said, "Were any names mentioned? Captain Peter Mark, Helen Sanchez? Wicek, Ortega, or Pelé?"

She shook her head. "I don't think Eddie ever knew anyone who wasn't named Joe or Fred or Mary."

"All right, Miss Radin, thank you," Beckett said.

Tucker said, "You can claim the body now."

"Claim?"

"To make the funeral arrangements," Tucker said.

"Yes," she said, stood up. "No one I know ever died. I guess his insurance will cover it."

At the office door she stopped. "He was working for Ben Scott—could I sue? I mean, Eddie was my only brother, he helped me out. You think Ben Scott owes me?"

"You could talk to a lawyer," Tucker said.

She nodded. "Ben Scott should pay me something."

*

Ben Scott woke up tired that Saturday. He lay looking out his bedroom windows at a twisted jacaranda with its feathery leaves and early blooms. It would be a good year for jacaranda.

He got out of bed and walked to the open French doors, the chill of a Southern California morning on his bare legs. He looked beyond the patio and pool to the small corral. He remembered when the main corrals had been moved away from the ranch house. *"We're not back-country ranchers any more, Benjamin,"* his father had said, *"We have a position in the county. The world's changing. Business and finance, that's the future, even for ranchers. We're branching out, putting our money into business and real estate. We'll be buying and selling land, not working it. You'll go East to school, learn how."*

East to school. To be a businessman, a city man, a desk man, and he had liked it, been good at it, enjoyed the status and the power, and yet somewhere inside, had always loved the slower pace of the land the way Roy had as a boy. Ben looked at Marlene asleep in her twin bed. He wished Roy had called him instead.

He stripped off his nightshirt, looked at his body in Marlene's full-length mirror. It wasn't much of a body even for an old man, pale and softly fat, a sagging belly and loose muscles. The price of power behind a desk—a power that, in time, seemed to lose its meaning. A body in pace with the land did not lose meaning. Was there still time? No, there was no time.

He began to dress in the rough ranch clothes Marlene hated him to wear. A negation of her needs? Clothes he wore more and more now. For an illusion of what he could be—a real rancher? Maybe there was time for that, but it would be time alone. He looked down at Marlene in the bed. Did he want to hold her? He still wanted to touch her, but that wasn't the same thing, and no one touched

Marlene unless she allowed it anyway—her time, her place, her way.

As he went out to the small corral, he wished again that Roy had come to him. He had a vision: Roy came to him, they got on their horses, rode into the silent canyons to the south. Into canyons where no one would find them. Alone with the hot land, the hawks, the vultures silent above.

He saddled his best horse and rode out across the fields. He had an hour before he had to dress for business.

*

The offices of Charro Ranch, Inc., were on the floor above Scott Real Estate Management. They told Beckett that Ben Scott would be in sometime before lunch.

Beckett drove to the Ambassador Hotel on an exclusive part of the beach front. Martin Elder had a second-floor suite. The oilman wasn't alone. Hamilton Scott was with him.

"Mr. Beckett, have you—?" the brother began.

"No. Have either of you heard from him?"

Hamilton shook his head. "If only Mother had taken me with her! You had him, and you lost him! If I could have talked to him, maybe I'd have learned what's wrong. All I can do is hang around the sheriff. I can't get near him!"

"I don't think he wants anyone near him," Beckett said.

Martin Elder said, "Someone had better find him. He could have killed Marlene in that cabin."

"Mr. Beckett?" Hamilton said, "is he really crazy? You talked to him. What did he say?"

"Let's say he's disturbed, blowing a lot of ways at once. Some are real, maybe, some aren't."

"Schizophrenic," Martin Elder said. "Dangerous."

Hamilton sat down, sagged. "Roy always wanted to figure it all out. I never saw much to figure, but I'm not smart like Roy. Trying to know too much can drive you nuts."

"It always has, Ham," Martin Elder said. "Take what you find and use it. Accept what is."

"I feel so damned helpless!" Hamilton said. "I even went to that Stella Ortega. Christ, what a hole she lives in. She said she hadn't seen Roy since that Monday night!"

"When did you go to Stella?"

"Yesterday. After Roy got away from you, I thought he'd maybe go to her, so I found her. There was a Helen Sanchez, too, and a Pelé something. They hadn't seen Roy, either."

Beckett said, "You know Edward Radin, Hamilton?"

"Radin?" Hamilton thought. "Isn't there a Radin who works for my father up in Monteverde? I don't know him."

"He did. He was the dead man in Roy's motel room."

Martin Elder said, "Your murder victim worked for Ben Scott? You're sure of that?"

"I'm sure," Beckett said. "It looks like Roy's mixed in a lot of different pressures. Suicide, drugs maybe, people after him, and maybe fraud right here."

"What about that possible fraud?" Martin Elder said.

"I came to ask you that. Your deal is still okay?"

"As far as I know. If anything is wrong, I don't know it, and neither does Hamilton," Elder said.

"Is that why Ham's here? To talk about your deal?"

"Partly," Elder said. "Ham's interested in the oil business, too. I wish more young people thought about business."

"Afraid for the future of the country?" Beckett said.

"Very afraid," Elder said. "Aren't you?"

"Sometimes," Beckett said.

*

Ben Scott was at work when Beckett got back to the offices of Charro Ranch, Inc. The businessman-rancher's face was as ruddy as if he'd been in the wind, but his eyes looked like he hadn't slept lately. He closed his office door behind Beckett, and walked to his desk. He didn't sit down. Beckett sat.

"Edward Radin," Beckett said.

Ben Scott picked up a paperweight. "So you found out."

"Why'd you lie, Mr. Scott?"

Ben Scott put down the paperweight. "I'm not really sure. Reflex. To have time to find out what had happened, maybe. Or maybe I couldn't make myself admit what I feared. What family can believe this has happened to them? I suppose I hoped that you'd find out that someone else had killed Radin before I had to connect Roy to him. I went up to Monteverde to see if Radin had told anyone up there anything. How could I tell what I knew, destroy my own son?"

"You know Roy's guilty? How?"

"Because I sent Radin after him, damn me!" The rancher sat down now, hunched forward. "The week Roy vanished, I decided to personally check out the land reports on the parcels I planned to sell to Martin Elder. A fluke, you see, just a whim. I found an odd fact—the mineral reports on some parcels were identical. That's just about impossible. I found that six parcels were old holdings, but six were new—bought only a month earlier! I located the land. It was useless land, no minerals near it, not even good grazing land!"

Ben Scott shook his head in disbelief. "The company we'd bought the land from turned out to be a dummy. No offices, a false address, the man who'd actually bought the land for the company had vanished. The land had been bought only a few weeks before it was sold to us. A swindle, pure and simple, with our own mineral reports used to do it!"

"Who was the man who bought the land?"

"He gave his name as Walter Payson, but there's no Payson like him listed in the directory, and no one ever heard of him," Ben Scott said. "But Roy had charge of those reports used in the swindle, and Roy's okay was on the purchase papers!"

"How much money?"

"About thirty thousand—in profit."

"Where did Edward Radin come in?"

"He was an expert on deeds and rights, I brought him down to check out every detail. He confirmed the fraud. Then I sent him to trace Roy. Radin knew every land dealer in the county, most in the state, and Roy didn't know him."

"It looks like Roy did know him. Is it all enough for murder, Scott? Would you have pressed charges?"

"No, but it couldn't be hidden, and there are laws,"

Ben Scott said. "You see, there's more. Radin found that some of the mineral reports had been tampered with, too. Not just copied. Land parcel numbers had been *added* to make the good reports appear to apply to additional land, then deleted. It could have only one purpose—to sell useless land to other people using our official reports to make the land seem rich. Our reports are like the Bible!"

Beckett nodded. "Your reputation used under the table to make greedy buyers think they were getting a steal. Honest buyers would check closer, but not marks hungry for a windfall. A classic con and swindle—the victim's greed is what makes a con work. Why would Roy do it?"

"Drug money, perhaps? An attack on me. Just an irrational game. It's not Roy, but Roy hasn't been like Roy."

"It's a fairly crude swindle," Beckett said.

"Not as much as it seems with hindsight. It could have taken years to discover in all my land, and there isn't any real proof of who did the faking inside my office—not legal proof. The only legal proof would come if those who bought the land talked. Aren't all swindles like that? If one victim talks, they fall apart, but no victim does talk?"

"That's how it works," Beckett admitted. "Except a real bunco man skips town fast. Roy couldn't do that."

"He ran to a hospital. Proving insanity, perhaps?" Ben Scott said. "If I hadn't spotted it, I might have sold the useless land to Martin Elder. Sooner or later it would have seemed as if I'd done the fraud! I'd have been accused.'"

Beckett said, "Roy told Dr. Remak he hated you."

Ben Scott said nothing.

"Was there enough money in it for a gang?" Beckett said.

"If it had gone on further."

"Is Roy the only one who could have done it all?"

"No," Ben Scott said, "I could have, and our office manager. Besides Roy, we have the only keys to the safe where those reports were. My office manager has been with me twenty years, lives alone with two grown daughters, doesn't need money, and is a church deacon."

"Hamilton? Your wife?"

"Neither my wife nor Hamilton needs money."

"You don't have to need money to want it," Beckett said.

"Hamilton doesn't even work in the office."

"Any angle for Martin Elder?"

Ben Scott looked out a window. "Not that I know of."

"Would your wife want to attack you for any reason?"

Scott looked back. "You don't mind what you suggest."

"Not in my job," Beckett said. "So it looks like Roy."

"Yes. That's why I got Radin, and got him killed!"

The small businessman looked out his windows again, his round face a study in pain.

Beckett rubbed at his jaw. "There's a pattern, you know?" he said. "Roy went into that car-arson as a kind of defiance, it looks like, conned by Ted Andrewski. There was another man in this swindle, maybe a pro, and he's vanished leaving Roy holding the bag."

There was hope on Ben Scott's soft face. "You think this other man could have killed Radin?"

"Maybe," Beckett said. "I can't see Roy murdering a man he knew was working for you. Only who knows what an irrational kid will do. He could have thought Radin was on his own, just a blackmailer. You said Roy didn't know Radin."

"I didn't think he did, no."

"But where would Ted Andrewski fit in?"

"I don't know," Ben Scott said.

"Did Radin tell you he'd found Roy?"

"No, but he did leave San Vicente that Sunday."

"Did Radin know Stella Ortega? Or Helen Sanchez?"

"I never heard him mention those names," Ben Scott said. "Could they have been in the swindle? Drug money?"

"Maybe. Radin might have found Roy through them. There's that hour missing from Stella Ortega's story, maybe she wasn't getting a shot. Then there's one more possibility—Howard Sill. Roy seems to have planned to contact him that Monday night."

Ben Scott was staring out his windows once more. "I don't know. Why would anyone else kill Radin, Beckett? I don't care how Radin found Roy. Did Roy kill him?"

Beckett shrugged, got up. "From your story, it looks like Roy. I hope there's a different story."

13

Howard Sill watched Beckett coming up the walk. The first husband of Marlene Scott leaned on a lawn-mower in the sun.

"The Saturday ritual?" Beckett said.

"What else?" Howard Sill said. "This afternoon I watch golf on TV. Dreams of Tahiti went long ago."

"With Marlene?"

"Later, when I knew why she'd left me," Sill said. "I was on my sixth job in four years, and all of a sudden I saw it. All I was ever going to do was work at small jobs in small towns. All repetition. I went out and got drunk. Then I married Sybil, got this house with her money, here we are."

"No more children?"

"Sybil can't. You haven't found Roy, Beckett?"

"I found him," Beckett said, "and lost him again."

He gave Sill a summary of the events in the Silver Camp cabin and the pass. The screen door at the side of the small house opened. Sybil Sill stood there. She didn't come out. She just stood in the doorway and watched Sill and Beckett on the grass in the sun. Howard Sill looked toward her.

"He's got a gun, he's all mixed up, and he's running out of space and time," Beckett said. "He could be in real danger, too. We know who the dead man was now. We don't know if Roy killed him or not. His name was Edward Radin."

Howard Sill leaned on the lawnmower, watched his wife silent in the doorway of his house. Beckett saw the struggle in the salesman's face. He waited. Howard Sill patted his shirt, found a cigarette, lit it, blew smoke into the sun.

"Radin came here last Sunday," Howard Sill said. "He was looking for Roy. We told him what we told you. Dr. Remak's name seemed to excite him."

"He'd talked to Ted Andrewski's wife. You should have told me earlier, Sill."

"Radin came from Ben Scott. We don't want any part of the Scotts, we mind our business. Roy isn't—" Howard Sill stopped, pushed at the lawnmower with his foot.

"There's something else?" Beckett said. "Roy did come to you on Monday night?"

"No," Sill said, "but he called me. At four in the morning! Sybil was mad. She's touchy about Marlene and Roy."

"What did he want? Or tell you?"

"Nothing. He was crazy, rambling. He said he just

had to talk to me, said he was healing wounds, mending fences—whatever that meant. Putting it in order, he said, with the honest people, the small people—like me! I guess that got me mad. No one likes to be told he's small even if he is. So I told him he was crazy. I told him to stay out of my life."

Sill blew smoke. "I didn't want to get involved with him, or with you. But that wasn't the whole reason I've kept shut. When you told me he'd been going to kill himself that night, I guess I felt guilty. I'd turned him away, hung up on him. Maybe he was calling people to talk him out of it. He's my kid, I should have talked, helped."

"Maybe you should have," Beckett said.

"Yeh," Sill said, and looked again toward where his wife still watched from the doorway. "Maybe a guy like me has to get scared to act. It's getting too mixed up. If you hadn't shown up today, I was coming to you anyway."

"Roy came to you in the last couple of days?"

Howard Sill nodded. "Wednesday night, bruised and bloody. He said he'd been in an accident. We let him stay the night. He left in the morning before I read about what happened to you in the pass. After I read about him escaping from you, I knew I should have turned him in that night. I don't think I could have, though. He's still my son."

"Ben Scott says the same."

"I guess he's got the right."

"Where had Roy been hiding? Where was he going?"

Howard Sill hesitated. "I don't want to make trouble."

"I've got a pretty good idea who hid him since Monday night: Helen Sanchez and Pelé Nascimento. I don't know where."

"In an old abandoned tool shack near the railroad tracks. They hid him behind junk, brought him food."

"Stella Ortega?"

"He said she had enough troubles without him."

"Did Edward Radin mention her name?"

"No."

"Where was Roy going when he left here Thursday morning?"

"He never said. I didn't ask him."

"Was he using drugs, Sill?"

"Not that I saw. Sybil gave him some of her codeine pain pills. They knocked him out fast. Guys on drugs don't get much effect from codeine pills, do they?"

"Not much. They made him sleep fast?"

Howard Sill nodded. "I went up once. He was sleeping hard, the way he did when he was a baby. Like sleep was safe."

*

Stella Ortega lay on the narrow bed in her bare room, the early afternoon sun slanting across her thin face, her hands flat at her sides. Helen Sanchez sat on a straight wooden chair.

"Easy, Stell," Helen said softly. "You can make it. In a few days you go to the clinic, okay?"

"Do I got to stay there, Helen?"

"After a few days you'll want to stay."

Stella's thin body arched, her mouth opened, but the spasm passed. She lay back as if surprised. "Hey, not so bad, you know?" A cold sweat beaded her brow. "No more'n like a baby comin'. Hey, maybe I have a baby to keep sometime, you know?"

"This is easier than a baby," Helen said. "No troubles after the pain's over. You don't have to feed it, or fight off rats. You get born yourself all over."

Helen looked at her watch in the bare little room. She lighted a cigarette. She smoked, and watched a dark shadow pass over the thin girl's face as another spasm racked her.

"It'll pass, baby," Helen said. "Ten more minutes."

The spasm passed, but not as fast this time. Stella lay breathing hard. She looked up at Helen with concern. "You got to get to work, Helen. I'm okay now."

"Not until two o'clock," Helen said. "Don't con me, baby. I know all the tricks, I used them all."

Stella turned her face to the wall. Time seemed to pass in the hot, bare room like a freight train across a desert, until, at last, Helen Sanchez got up and went to a milk bottle full of orange juice. She poured juice up to a mark on a glass, brought the glass to Stella Ortega.

Stella stared. "*Dios!* Orange juice!"

"Drink it, baby."

Stella drank, her hands shaking. She lay back. Helen sat in the chair.

Stella began to breathe more easily. "I . . . I feel nice," she said. "A lil' high. Like I had a hit maybe half hour ago. I feel . . . okay."

"It's a high like H, only milder. Give it time and it fills the need, and leaves you okay to work, eat, sleep."

Stella's eyes shone. "It's okay, Helen, you know? I can do it! Right here! I don' need no clinic!"

"Not so simple, Stell. Not alone. It hooks you, too, but with help you can kick it easier—a lot easier. But you got to have a program and a doctor. I'll come back for two more doses. Tomorrow you'll feel relaxed, but it's only a start. You have to come to the clinic."

"I'm scared, Helen. The cops—"

"Most of us in the program know the Man like a brother."

Stella smiled. "Maybe if I kick . . . maybe me and Roy—?"

"Think about it," Helen said. "Think about Roy. Think hard, baby. You can have someone like that someday. Maybe not Roy, but there's plenty of Roys want a pretty girl."

Stella's laugh was shy, soft. "I always like Roy, you know? In the motel, Monday, he was real nice. Sort of soft 'n thinking about *me*. On'y . . . he was gonna kill himself, Helen. I know. He in bad, bad trouble."

"I figured to kill myself fifty times," Helen said. "I never did. Roy can get out of it. So can you, baby."

"Helen?" Stella said. "Roy, he don' kill no one. I know."

Helen Sanchez watched the thin girl. "You know where Roy is right now, honey?"

"Me? I don' know where he is!"

"You're sure, baby?" Helen studied Stella's thin face. "I been after you six months to try the treatment. How come you say yes now?"

"What else I do? The cops're watchin' me all the time."

"You're in no shape, honey. If you hide Roy, the cops—"

Stella said, "Hey, how about me and Roy someday? What a crazy dream, you know?"

"Why not? He's a man."

"Hey, now who cons?"

"I'm the expert," Helen said. "Besides, it's no con. Roy's not like his family. You think I'd like him, help him, if he was like the others? Now you rest, try to sleep. I'll be back in time for the next dose."

"I sleep 'n dream about Roy 'n me!"

"Go, baby," Helen said.

Stella closed her eyes. She felt warm and liquid in the hot room, her legs floating in some thick, slow fluid. She saw Helen smiling down at her above the bed.

"Hey," Stella said, "I think big. Roy Scott."

"Why not, baby," Helen said, "why not?"

Helen . . . but it wasn't Helen's voice. The room was empty. Helen was gone.

"Why not, baby?" the same voice said.

It was Stella's own voice. She was talking to herself. She must have been asleep. How long? She looked at the window. The sun was still high in the early afternoon. Just a doze, and Stella closed her eyes once more, let herself slip down into the soft liquid that flowed all through her.

The knock on the door was light.

"What?" Stella said.

Was she asleep? No, her eyes were open. The sun was high.

The knock came again.

Stella sat up. "Who . . . who is it?"

The voice was low, urgent. "Stella? It's me, Roy!"

"Roy?" She got up, hurried to the door, opened it. "What you do here when you got to hide and—?"

The slender man came into the room fast. Stella screamed. The man held a long-barreled pistol. A young man with hard, cool eyes.

"No more noise, Miss Ortega," Captain Peter Mark said.

*

Beckett saw the old blue Ford in the rooming-house yard, and went up the stairs to 2-D. Helen Sanchez opened the door. She was dressed to go out. Beckett pushed inside. No one else was there. He turned on Helen Sanchez.

"You slipped me Wednesday. Where'd you go? You can't go far, not you three."

"Why can't we go far, Mr. Beckett?"

"Don't fool with me! I know you hid Roy on Tuesday and Wednesday. For fix money? He had money. You're a known addict, you hid a fugitive. You know what that means for you?"

She sat down in the neat living-room section of the room. Beckett never took his eyes from her. She looked at her room.

"Don't you ever change?" she said to Beckett. "Drugs on your brain, so you don't see. Look at this room. You ever see an addict's pad like this? Did you find any junk here?" She bared her right arm. It was mottled with old needle scars—but all old. "If we hid Roy, it wasn't for fix money."

Beckett looked at her arm, and around at the neat room with its bright Mexican throws, its clean surfaces, its repaired furniture, and its food in plain sight—good, fresh food.

"You're saying you're clean now? Pelé, too? No! Your kind never stops. You hid Roy Scott from the police."

"We hid him," Helen Sanchez said. "He came here around six A.M. that Tuesday morning. He was in a daze. He talked about suicide and murder. He didn't make sense, and he was passing out. We hid him two days, fed him, then he ran out on us. He had a car, he took it and ran. We don't know where."

"Two days? He was in that shack all day Wednesday?"

"Up to maybe five o'clock. We checked every hour."

Beckett thought. Then he said, "Can I take an addict's word? Tell me about your miracle cure, Helen."

"No miracle," Helen Sanchez said. "There's no miracles for slum kids been on the stuff since fourteen. No life, either. You're a junkie and you're poor, then you got to be a thief, a con artist, a hustler. A year ago me and Pelé was up to the judge sixteen times each. We were dead, gone, down the drain all the way. Pelé he says one day, like that, it got to end. Pelé's strong. Maybe because he was an athlete, I don't know. But he wakes up that day, and he says it got to stop or it's zero. So he went to the clinic."

"Clinic?" Beckett said. "Free drugs?"

She shrugged. "Cops and nice people, you know all about putting us in jail, but not much about how to help. They got a clinic here. Two docs and a preacher. Methadone therapy. Pelé joined up, and he meant it. I had to make my choice."

She found a cigarette on a table, lighted it, looked at her steady hands. "My whole life was scheming. Tired all the time. When I was a kid I worked the good hotels, but I'd lost so much weight, was so beat-up, the last years all I could do was work cheap bars, walk streets. No days, only nights. I never saw the sun except through shades in some dirty room no one ever cleaned, especially not me. Then Pelé went to the clinic. He began to make it. He got some health back, got a real job, started school to learn car repair. I saw how it had to be. I had to give up the drugs, or give up Pelé."

Through the smoke of her own cigarette, her somber eyes showed the remembered labyrinth of that choice. "I knew Pelé was all I really had, all I really wanted, so I went to the clinic. In ten days I put on ten pounds. I relaxed for the first time in almost twenty years. No miracle; it took a while, and it took a lot of help. I walk past my old bars, and I still shiver after a year. I see my old friends down on Nopal Street in Needle Park, and I can feel the pull down to my shoes, but I pass them by. I say to myself, God, I want that kick! But I say, too, God, I'm glad I'm not there any more."

She looked again around the small, neat room with its orderly little roomlike areas, just as in any real home. "I can eat. Real food—meat, potatoes, vegetables, milk, bread, ice cream. A year ago I couldn't have kept a plate of it down. A year ago we were dead, zero. Now me and Pelé are going to get married. Maybe get a real apartment someday. We work now. I hold the same job nine months now. We had no more time to throw away. Nobody's long enough to live with drugs."

Beckett waited for her to go on, but she didn't. She'd told all she had to tell. The rest of the story was in the future. Beckett looked at the room again. The truth of her story was in that room. If nothing else, the truth was there in all the small possessions no addict would ever have because he would have sold them long ago for drug money. The truth of her story—so far. What was the final truth?

"No backsliding?" Beckett said. "You hid a man wanted for suspicion of murder. Why, Helen?"

"I told you, he is a friend. You live your life in gutters at midnight, you know friends got to be helped. That's all. We talked, me and Pelé. We say no, we can't risk it. It's too much to ask. We'll lose all we made in a year of sweat. We tell ourselves no, we got to turn away." She shrugged, her intelligent eyes aware of both the stupidity and necessity of the decision. "But we can't turn away. We can't send Roy away, he needs the help. We have run all our lives, now Roy is running. We do not think he has killed, we must help."

"No matter what it costs you?"

"We were afraid. We hoped no one would know. If we lose, then we will pay. Maybe we will make it, who knows?"

"Where is Roy now, Helen? Tell me, and maybe—"

Beckett didn't hear the door open, or the man behind him. An arm clamped around his throat, a hand pressed behind his head. A judo hold. He couldn't move. One move and he could break his own neck like the snapping of a chicken's neck.

"Pelé! Stop it!" Helen Sanchez cried.

The voice was close in Beckett's ear. "He will send us to jail! We're not losing it all!"

The voice, and his own blood, hammering in Beckett's ear. Pelé's face close to the back of his neck, breathing hard.

"We knew, honey," Helen said, her eyes fixed on the face Beckett couldn't see behind him.

"If I kill him, who will know? They will say Roy—"

Helpless, Beckett hung in Pelé's hands like an insect on a pin, the victim in the mandibles of an ant.

Helen said, "Not like that. No, Pelé. No more like that."

Beckett hung there, the breath on his neck. His blood in his ears throbbed the seconds. Then the pressure was gone.

Beckett whirled, his hand reaching toward the pistol on his belt. Pelé Nascimento stood in the room with empty hands. Beckett did not draw his gun.

"We don't fight that way any more," Helen Sanchez said. "We do not know where Roy is now, not since Wednesday evening. If you want to arrest us for hiding him those two days, we will be here. This is our home. We have jobs. We won't run."

Her voice had a certain pride in it—she had a home. The pride of any normal person who had never lived in the twilight world of drugs and the endless crimes to feed those drugs. She would not run, neither of them would, no more than any good citizens on their safe streets, in their safe homes. Pride now, if they went to jail once more for it.

"Who else would hide Roy?" Beckett said.

"There must be many," Helen said. "His family, his brother."

Pelé said, looking only at Helen, "Stella isn't at her pad, Helen. I went by five minutes ago."

"She has to be," Helen said. "I left her there only a half hour ago. She had her methadone, she was okay!"

"She's gone now," Pelé said. "Her door is open, and her car is gone."

Beckett said, "Was she supposed to be there?"

"Yes, waiting for me," Helen said. "I'm giving her the methadone. She's afraid of the clinic. I thought that if I could show her it would work, she'd come to the clinic." She shook her head. "I've been after her for six months. All of a sudden she wanted to try. She talks of Roy and herself, Mr. Beckett, as if suddenly she is closer to him."

"Could she be hiding him now?"

"It'd be a crazy risk for both of them," Pelé said. "The cops know all about Stella, been watching her."

"You all got away from me, and maybe Roy had nowhere else to go," Beckett said. "When he escaped in the pass, he knew I knew about you two, about the Silver Camp cabin, and I don't think he trusts his family. Ther Janice Rhine, and I think he did call her, but she' amilton's girl—risky. He might have tried Stel, and she might have hidden him if she had somewhere safer than her room. Is there anywhere?"

Helen Sanchez said, "Her brother's house. It's over in Fremont. He's a fisherman, lives alone. He's out on a tuna boat now, won't be back for a month."

"What's the address?"

They told him.

14

Fremont is the third largest city in Buena Costa County. On the coast, twenty miles north of San Vicente, it is an industrial city with neither mountains nor beauty. A grimy city of fishing fleets, canneries, fertilizer factories, and oil refineries, it clusters around a smoky, oil-polluted harbor. A mile north of the city there are petro-chemical plants, and lighter industry fills the outlying areas.

A town of treeless streets, cheap tract houses, shabby bars and bowling alleys for the workers. For the managers, there is one country club and golf course, and to swim, the managers and the few rich go four miles down to Cuyama Beach.

Beckett found the house of Stella Ortega's brother on a broken-down street in a sparse section of the city near a refinery. A peeling frame cottage set far back from the street, the freeway close behind it. There were no cars in front or at the sides, and all the shades were down.

Beckett parked out of sight from the house, and walked back. As he passed he saw a pot of geraniums broken near the front door, and heard a radio blaring loud rock music from inside. When he was out of sight once more, he circled to approach the house from the side. Stella Ortega's green Mustang was parked at the rear hidden from the street.

Beckett drew his pistol, slipped in under a side window, and raised up. The shade was down, but there was a thin gap at the bottom. He saw a piece of wall and floor, a ____ couch, the corner of an open doorway, and the legs of a seated woman. The woman's legs were tied to the chair she sat in. No one moved in the room, and he heard nothing except the violent radio and the traffic on the freeway.

He went around to the front door. It was ajar. He pushed it open and stepped into a shaded room. The woman tied to the chair was Stella Ortega. Her face was bruised, and drying blood trickled from her slack mouth. Her eyes were open, but dilated, seeing nothing. Her dress had been torn down, and narrow cuts bled all across her bird-thin shoulders. Her bare feet had been burned.

Low moans came from her slack mouth. She seemed unaware of the sounds she was making. Her head was slumped sideways as if there were no bone in her neck.

Beckett went to her. "Stella? Who did it? Did they want Roy?"

She tried to jerk her head up as if trying to escape from his voice, but it slumped forward on her limp neck. Beckett reached out to raise her head.

The hard metal object slammed against his head from behind. He hit the floor on his face, raised to turn and see who had hit him, and fell flat again.

*

A shaft of dusty sunlight slanted through a hole in a drawn shade. There was no sound anywhere. Beckett tried to sit up. He couldn't. His hands were tied behind him, his feet lashed.

He lay breathing slowly. His head was sore but clear. He had no headache. Unconscious only a few moments, and still in the same room. The sounds of the freeway became audible. The radio was silent. Stella Ortega?

Beckett tried to see her. He couldn't from where he lay. He tested his bonds. They were tight, but by heaving his body, crawling, he managed to inch his way up to a sitting position against a wall. His knees stabbed pain, his shoulder throbbed.

Stella Ortega was in the same chair. Her head was down on her chest.

"Stella?" Beckett said.

She didn't answer.

"Stella, can you move at all?"

Her mouth was still open, but twisted and rigid now, as if from some massive shock inside. She was absolutely still. Her chest didn't move. Without seeing her face, or touching her, Beckett knew that she was dead.

*

Beckett was still looking at the dead girl when he heard the footsteps come into the room. Roy Scott stood just inside the doorway. He held a pistol, and he looked at Stella Ortega. Then he came toward Beckett.

"I had to hit you," Roy said. "You came in while I was with Stella. I'm sorry."

"Who killed her, Roy?"

Roy squatted down beside Beckett. "I did," he said. "I'll check those ropes, make sure they're not too tight."

"Why did you kill her?" Beckett said.

Roy stood up. "I didn't know I was going to. She hid me here, so she's dead. I think she wanted me, so she's dead. You can't escape killing, you know? One way or the other, you kill. In the army, in a car, in a jury box, in an office that won't hire a man. In the police. When you pay taxes. Just by being alive in this world. If I was dead, Stella'd be alive."

"Stella hid you here? Someone came after you by using her, and then killed her?"

Roy said, "It doesn't matter what you decide to do. It doesn't help to stay out, do nothing. They made her bring them here, and they hurt her. They hurt her!"

He went to the dead girl. "You know what she did? She knocked over a flower pot out front so I'd see it and know someone was here. She knew I was only out for food, so she warned me. She didn't tell them, so she's dead."

"She was alive when I came in, Roy," Beckett said. "No one was here except you."

"I saw them come out," Roy said. "They walked out just like human beings. They drove off. I came inside. When you arrived I had to hit you."

He looked down at Stella Ortega. Then he turned and began to walk quickly toward the outside door.

Beckett said, "Who walked out of here, Roy?"

Roy stopped as if Beckett's voice were a long arm

that reached to hold him. He stood like a robot that must respond, must do what it is commanded to do.

"Them," he said. "Once I saw Captain Mark push two Cong out of a helicopter because they wouldn't spit on each other when he told them to. He chopped the head off a girl he caught stealing beer from his storehouse. Wicek kills only for his money, but Mark likes to kill. He's afraid of death."

His voice went distant, dreamlike. "I wanted to know all about it. I found out, and I told. They said I had no proof, just my unsupported word. They said they knew all about it, but there wasn't enough proof. They said that was the way it was, I should forget it. So I forgot. Only—"

There was a silence. Roy started for the door again.

"Roy," Beckett said, "cut me loose!"

Roy Scott went out through the door, pulled it locked.

*

Beckett still sat against the wall. The sun was gone. No one had heard his shouts.

Stella Ortega hung dead in her chair.

In the growing darkness, there was nothing for Beckett to do but wait and think. He thought about Captain Peter Mark, and about Sergeant Anton Wicek, who was obviously, now, the other man with Captain Mark on the beach near the Sierra Motel. They wanted Roy Scott badly enough to take big risks, expose themselves. He thought about a dark man in a yellow car who had trailed Roy Scott on Monday. Not Edward Radin, no—Radin had been a blond.

He thought about Ted Andrewski, who had talked to Roy in the hospital, and who was now dead. He thought about Edward Radin and a crude swindle.

Time crawled. He shouted. No one came.

It was full night, Stella Ortega's body barely visible in the dark room, when the car stopped outside.

Two people came up the walk. The front door rattled. The footsteps went around to the rear. Someone was in the kitchen. The lights went on in the living room. Hamilton Scott stood with his hand on the light switch. His other hand was empty. Marlene Scott was behind him. Beckett watched them.

Marlene said, "Roy called Hamilton, he said you—"

She saw Stella Ortega, choked a scream, her hand to her face. Hamilton's face went green as he saw the dead girl.

"Cut me loose," Beckett said.

Hamilton found a knife in the kitchen. Freed, Beckett massaged his wrists, stamped his numbed feet.

"Roy called me on my private line at the ranch," Hamilton said. "I guess he wanted only me. He told me where you were, told me to free you. He sounded all crazy. Mother made me bring her, too."

Marlene Scott said, "I thought he might be here. I thought that this time—" She looked at Stella. "Did Roy—?"

"Maybe," Beckett said. "Did he say where he was?"

"No, nothing," Hamilton said. "I thought maybe you'd know something, Mr. Beckett. If he told you anything at all, maybe I could help figure out where he is."

"He told me nothing. Call the police, Ham."

The detective-lieutenant of the Fremont police took the descriptions of Roy Scott, Captain Peter Mark, and Sergeant Anton Wicek. He also took Beckett's story.

"I'll report anything to Tucker," the lieutenant said.

"That's it," Beckett said. "Tucker only, but they won't hang around here."

The assistant coroner stood up from where he had been working over Stella Ortega. He was pale as he wiped his hands. "She was tortured, beaten and cut. That didn't kill her, though." He glanced at Beckett. "She was an addict?"

"Yes," Beckett said.

The coroner nodded. "I can't be certain until the autopsy, but I'd say she died from an overdose of heroin. A big overdose. Not the kind of r   e an addict would be likely to make on her own."

The Fremont lieutenant said, "We haven't found any syringe or heroin in the house."

"So someone gave her the dose. Murder," Beckett said. "How long would it have taken to kill her?"

"Maybe ten or fifteen minutes. She'd have been out almost at once, barely conscious. I'll get you the full report."

"Send it to Prosecutor Tucker," Beckett said. "I'll leave the rest up to you here, Lieutenant."

The lieutenant said, "I'll need a formal statement from the kid and his mother. The telephone call and all."

"Hamilton will give it to you, I didn't talk to my son," Marlene said. "I want to go with Mr. Beckett."

"You better stay with Hamilton," Beckett said.

"Can't we all go?" Hamilton said. "What can I tell—?"

"I need the statement," the lieutenant said.

"I'll go back with Mr. Beckett, Hamilton," Marlene said. "You have the car. Don't argue with me!"

Hamilton said nothing more.

Beckett went to the front door. "Come on, then, Mrs. Scott," he said.

She followed him out.

*

The road was dark in the early night hours, the head-lights of Beckett's car picking out trees and silent houses that seemed to leap out of the night as he drove fast toward San Vicente. Marlene Scott sat beside him, closer to him than she had to, as if she needed the touch of a human body. Her crystal façade had cracked now, and she looked soft and very beautiful—a woman and vulnerable.

"What is he going to do, Mr. Beckett?" she said, even her voice softened, the voice of a mother afraid for her son. "I . . . I was sure it was all . . . nothing. Some . . . mistake. Even at that cabin. Just disturbed, agitated, at sea over nothing, the way he always was. Something in-side him that was never content, always pacing inside him-self like a caged lion. Now . . . Is he insane, Mr. Beckett? Did he murder that girl? Is he going to . . . kill again?"

"I don't think he killed Stella, and maybe not any-one," Beckett said, his eyes fixed on the dark road. "I don't know what he's going to do. I don't think he's sure. But I think he might get killed himself if we don't find him."

"Killed?" she said, shivered close to Beckett.

Beckett was aware of her body beside him. Suddenly, out of nowhere, and no part of the killings or the case, he was alert to her as a woman. It had been a long time since he'd thought about a woman, and the uncontrolled response was something he could neither stop nor ignore.

She said, "What is it all about, Mr. Beckett?"

"My name's Lee," he said. "It's about something that went on over in Vietnam. Something that Roy got mixed in. At least, part of it is. I'm not sure about all of it."

"Vietnam? What would Roy be mixed in? He's only a boy. He was just a soldier!"

"He's a special kind of boy," Beckett said. "There's a pattern to his actions. Janice Rhine said it—he's a boy who was *looking,* finding out, trying to understand his world and what choices he had in it for his life. All you had to do was look at him and listen, Marlene."

"I listened! I did! Roy never made any sense to me!"

"You listened, but you didn't hear," Beckett said. "Maybe you couldn't. Neither you nor Ben Scott. Roy dropped out of two colleges because he didn't find the answers he wanted. He found them, or some of them, at the university here. But what he found clashed with what his father, Ben, that is, told him, and he was close to Ben, listened to him, right?"

She nodded. "Yes. As a boy they were very close. Much closer than Roy ever was to me."

"So when he graduated he was confused—between what he had learned at the university and what Ben had taught him. He went to Vietnam to 'get the real picture' for himself, he said that. Over there he watched, looked, learned—he did it actively, I think, like a crusader. What he learned did something to him, and at least some part of it was real and dangerous."

Beckett stopped to pass a slow-moving car. He lit a cigarette, smoked as the trees jumped past in the glare of his headlights. "Roy's an abstract man, a theorizer, and I don't think he realized the real danger of what he knew. I think he pulled into a shell, rejected the world and any action, and came home detached, mentally isolated inside himself—until some incident a month ago triggered a violent reaction that both drove him irrational and into some kind of action."

"Incident? What incident?"

"You should know that, Marlene, not me," Beckett said.

"But I don't, Lee! Unless . . . that arson?"

"The arson is part of it," Beckett said, "but my hunch says that was a result, not the cause."

Marlene was silent, her classic face under the smooth blond hair fixed straight ahead. "How does it happen, Lee? I tried to give him a good life, everything a boy should have. He had a fine home, advantages. Each of my marriages gave us a better life. Ben loved him from the start. It was always Roy that Ben liked most. Two boys, and one turns out strong and solid, happy with his life, and the other is all trouble and anguish."

Beckett said, "Some people are born more sensitive to their world. They have to understand, not accept."

"Understand what, Lee? You try to make the best life for yourself, have everything you can. Everyone does."

"Not everyone," Beckett said. "But maybe Roy is in danger now from some people who do want everything."

"Is that where we're going? To find who wants to hurt Roy, who's doing all this?"

"It's where I'm going. You're going to the ranch."

She leaned against him. "No, I can't go to the ranch. Ben's away again, I'd be alone. That's why I came with

Ham, really. I didn't want to be alone out there. Ham didn't want to take me, but I made him, and you have to take me, too. Please, Lee."

He was aware of her body. "Can't you call Martin Elder?"

She didn't pull away. "He's busy. Tonight I want to go with you. I have a right to know why all this is happening."

Ahead, the county road joined the freeway just outside San Vicente. The lights of the city were in sight. But Beckett knew that he wanted her with him, for himself.

"All right," he said.

He drove onto the freeway ramp, and turned south away from San Vicente.

15

Dr. Emil Remak worked alone in the study of his new house on the hill. He seemed oblivious to the distant sound of the television in the living room, but each time the telephone rang he grabbed it as if his work wasn't really in his mind. It rang three times in an hour, and Remak swore softly under his breath—colleagues with small problems. He spoke briefly to them, and after the third call, pushed his work away.

He went to his study windows. In the clear night the sea was darkly visible through a gap in the hills. Far out a fog bank was moving slowly toward the land. The May fog getting ready for morning. He was still at the windows, watching the distant fog, when the car came up the hill and stopped in his turnaround.

Remak started for the door of the study, then stopped. He went back and sat behind his desk. He picked up a report, but sat alert and listening. Almost five minutes passed. Remak fidgeted in his chair, started to get up again, when, at last, the doorbell rang.

"Emil," his wife called from outside the study, "someone to see you. Are you free?"

"Send them in, Sybil," Remak called out.

He half-stood as the door opened, and then sat slowly down again. Lee Beckett from San Vicente came in with a blond woman. Beckett closed the door behind them. Dr. Remak nodded to the big man and the blond woman.

"You've found him, Mr. Beckett?" Remak said.

"Twice," Beckett said, "and lost him again both times. This is Mrs. Marlene Scott, Roy's mother."

"I'm sorry to meet you under these conditions, Mrs. Scott," Remak said. "Roy told me a great deal about you."

"That he hated me, Dr. Remak?" Marlene said.

Remak sighed unhappily. "You must understand that Roy is disturbed. His hates and loves are all part of his irrational condition. They are true, yes, but not necessarily real. You understand? He hates an abstract fantasy he has of you."

Beckett, who had not sat down, stood now just inside the door in shadows away from the desk, and said, "What about his condition that's both true and real, Dr. Remak?"

"In a sense, all his problems are very real, too, Mr. Beckett," Remak explained. "That doesn't mean they're not a kind of fantasy."

Beckett stepped closer to the desk. "The trouble I mean isn't fantasy. It's real trouble, Remak, and it made you follow Roy from the hospital to the Sierra Motel on Monday."

The change in Dr. Emil Remak wasn't visible, but it was there. Remak was a trained psychiatrist schooled to face almost any surprise without visible reaction, but it wasn't a patient he was facing now, and his left hand jerked twice as he watched Beckett.

Beckett leaned with his hands flat on the desk. "When I told you about the dead man in the Sierra, you assumed it was Roy because you expected him to be found dead!" Beckett said. "Not just because he was suicidal, but because you knew someone was chasing him. You knew that—because you'd tailed Roy, found him, and then sent someone after him. You wanted Roy dead, Remak, so much that when you found out he wasn't dead, you tried to make Captain Deraita and me think he was so dangerous we'd shoot him on sight!"

Dr. Remak seemed to draw into a tight, rigid shell in his chair, hunched and leaning toward Beckett. "Roy is dangerous!" he said.

"To you, maybe, but not to me or any policeman. He had a chance to shoot me cold, and he didn't. He let me take him rather than shoot me, Remak. He may be suicidal, I think he is, but he's not homicidal—except to those who are a danger to *him*. A real danger, not fantasy."

Remak hunched tighter, as if in a cold wind, as if he saw monsters around him in the shadows of his own study.

Beckett said, "We just stopped to look into your garage. The Continental is there, and a green Pontiac. A brand-new Pontiac with a temporary license. Your wife's car, right? Only it's not the car she had on Monday, is it? No, that was a yellow car—the car you used to follow Roy to San Vicente. After I asked about what car you drove, you sold the yellow car, but it won't be hard to prove."

Remak said, "I sold it. It was wrong for Sybil. I bought a new one while I could get a good trade-in."

Beckett shook his head. "It won't work, Remak. The manager at the Sierra remembers you, and he'll know you when he sees you. Other people you talked to on Monday will remember when they see you in a police line-up. Then the car will mean plenty."

Dr. Emil Remak said nothing this time. He only watched Beckett the way a rabbit watches an owl about to swoop.

Beckett straightened up, looked all around the good study. "This is an expensive new house for an ex-army doctor on VA pay now. I expect we'll find that you've got a lot more money than you can really explain. You've probably got it well hidden, but the government can dig it out when I tell them all about you, and Anton Wicek and Captain Peter Mark."

"Wicek?" Dr. Remak said. "Captain Mark? You—"

"I spotted them, Doctor. In fact, they came to me. I guess they're really desperate, just as you were. Captain Mark is a pretty young man to have the money to buy a business partnership, and West Pointers don't quit the army without a hell of a reason."

Like a balloon with a slow leak, Remak came out of his hunched shell. His body relaxed, and he sat up in his chair like a man out from under a weight. As if he was relieved to face, at last, a specific accusation. "I don't know what you're talking about," he said.

Beckett said, "I'm talking about greed, the big money. About Captain Peter Mark—a man who wants everything, that's what Roy said, and he seems to know.

Captain Peter Mark, who was three years in Vietnam and who has plenty of money now that he's out of the army. About Anton Wicek, and Roy and you—all of you in Vietnam. What was it, Remak? Black market? Drug smuggling? Both?"

Remak shook his head back and forth over and over. He didn't answer this time, he just shook his head, denying, and looked toward Marlene Scott as if she would tell Beckett the truth for him.

"Peter Mark, a man who wants it all," Beckett said, "and a killer who likes to kill, that's what Roy said. A killer who's killed a girl who just helped Roy, and probably Andrewski right here in your hospital, and a nobody named Edward Radin who just got in the way at the wrong time! Captain Mark and Sergeant Wicek—and you, Remak. You're part of it, and when we catch them, they'll talk—especially Wicek."

"No," Remak said, somehow unable to stop looking at Marlene Scott. "No."

"You're the link between Roy and them. There's no one else," Beckett said. "Maybe you didn't know they'd kill anyone, but you better help now, or you're as guilty as they are."

Emil Remak blinked at Beckett in silence. "No," he said at last, "I never thought they'd kill anyone. All they were supposed to do was bring Roy back, and if he wouldn't see reason, I could certify him insane. That was all!"

"Black market, Doctor? In Vietnam—and Roy knew about it? When he came to you this time he was going to blow the whistle?"

Remak nodded. "Yes. Black market. We . . . we

made a fortune, each of us. We thought we were safe, it was all in the past and far away. Then Roy came. Ruin and jail, both!"

"A beautiful war," Beckett said. "Who cares who wins? Everyone comes out rich—except the dead soldiers, and those dead another way. What did Roy know? How did he know? What made him suddenly dangerous when he hadn't been before?"

Remak hunched over again in his chair, reliving the fear and the danger. "Roy was sent to my psychiatric unit in Saigon. Battle fatigue, badly shaken. He had very good contacts on the line in the north, was bitter against the army, was intelligent and dependent on me in the hospital. We were diverting some medical supplies, and . . ."

"A pretty racket," Beckett said.

"Extra supplies!" Remak said. "I overrequisitioned, no one was hurt by it. The Vietnamese needed medical—"

"No one hurt," Beckett said. "Just money."

Remak shrugged. He seemed to have grown smaller in the last few minutes. "I needed someone who could move around, just to be careful, not on the staff. Roy seemed good, so I had Wicek contact him, explain the setup. Roy seemed to agree, and Wicek sent him to Captain Mark. For a time it went fine, Roy even made some money for himself; his treatment in my ward was perfect cover. Then—"

Remak hunched even smaller in his chair. "Then Roy tried to inform on our whole operation. He didn't get far, of course, everyone knows the black market exists. If it hadn't been us, it would have been someone else."

"Simple business, get your share," Beckett said.

16

Prosecutor Tucker was still in his office that Saturday night. His staff was busy, and his phones rang even at midnight. Torture-murders of women didn't happen often in Buena Costa County, not with known suspects to be hunted and newspapers waiting for bulletins.

Beckett walked into the office with Marlene Scott.

"Where the hell have you been?" Tucker demanded.

"Busy," Beckett said. "The Fremont cops filled you in on what I told them about Stella Ortega's killing?"

Tucker nodded, pointed to the map of the county on his wall. "We've got the county sealed off: airports, train stations, bus depots, highways. Thank God for the mountains. They leave only four decent ways out of the county by car."

"Unless they walk through the mountains," Beckett said. "They're soldiers."

"You're sure Captain Mark and Wicek killed her, not Roy?" Tucker said it, and flushed as he looked at Marlene. "I'm sorry, Mrs. Scott, but I have to consider everything."

"I know what you have to do," Marlene said.

Beckett said, "I'm not sure of anything, Charley. We better find Roy Scott, too, and fast."

He gave Tucker the details of what Dr. Emil Remak had told. Tucker listened with his eyes growing animated, his lips wet, like a hungry lion that has just discovered a herd of zebra in plain sight.

When Beckett finished, Tucker sat down slowly. "A black market ring so successful most of its members are safe out of the army? Doctors and West Pointers? Damn, but it's big, Lee. Washington'll be in it. International!"

"Maybe, Charley, but we can work while we're waiting for the FBI and the Associated Press. Right now it's local. I don't know who killed Stella for sure, but I do know who gets killed next if we don't find Roy Scott."

"You think Mark and Wicek want to kill Roy?" Tucker said.

"I'm sure of it, and they're trained killers. Maybe Roy is out of the county by now, but I doubt it, and Captain Mark will be where he is. They all know we're after them, and our total force isn't big for a whole county. Mark and Wicek are smart, trained men used to staying safe, and no one knows them in the county except me. Most of your men, and Hoag's, don't know what they're looking for. All they have to do is hole up."

"Roy, maybe," Tucker said, "but the other two have to move around to find him."

"They found Stella Ortega without being spotted. They know what they're doing. Any clues in Wicek's hotel room?"

"Nothing," Tucker said. "We have to hope for a break."

"Breaks take time we don't have," Beckett said. He looked at both Tucker and Marlene Scott. "Where would Roy go? Stella Ortega's dead. Helen Sanchez and Pelé would be too risky, and so would Howard Sill now. I don't think Roy would go to them anyway, not after what happened to Stella for hiding him. The cabin at Silver Camp is known by us. About all he has left is the ranch and the family, maybe Janice Rhine."

"Or the mountains," Marlene Scott said. She sat down now. "Why doesn't he come for help? He must know they're after him?"

Beckett shook his head. "He won't give himself up. You have to face that whether he killed anyone or not, he's not rational. He knows his danger, but he doesn't care. He's suicidal, yet he's running to stay alive, too—a kind of irrational instinct. He wants to be dead, but he can't bring himself to die. There's a very human difference between the condition of death and the act of dying. I think there's something about danger that makes him fight, and he's in psychic limbo."

"Then what will he do, Lee?" Marlene asked.

"I'm not sure he knows himself. Reach for the past, maybe. You say that Ben's been away all day?"

"Yes," Marlene said. "Looking for Roy, I think. Hoping."

"Roy might just go to Ben now," Beckett said. "He's

an animal being doubly hunted, he might go home all the way, to his childhood. I'll go with you to the ranch, Marlene."

"Hoag and I'll go on after Captain Mark and Wicek," Tucker said, his eyes excited like a hound's on the scent of a big one. "We'll flush them sooner or later."

"Yeh," Beckett said. "In a day or two the odds are on our side, but right now the odds favor Captain Mark. We're going to need some luck, and so is Roy Scott."

*

Roy Scott crouched in the dark night of the Charro Ranch. He was hidden in thick manzanita a hundred yards from Janice Rhine's house, a silent shadow in the night.

From time to time his hand moved as if looking for something that should have been there. The rifle that had always been there in the hotter Vietnam nights. His brain hadn't thought about the rifle, but his hand had a better memory.

He had been hidden for some hours when he saw the boy. No more than twelve, the boy appeared from the dirt road and took up a position in the shadow of a corral fence post.

Roy Scott watched for another half hour. The boy just sat there by the fence, watching the Rhine house. Roy stood and glided silently over a small hill. A shaggy horse stood tied to a tree. Roy mounted the horse and rode away across the fields of the big ranch in the darkness.

*

The ranch house was dark when Marlene opened the door. She switched on the lights, led Beckett into the living room. Beckett sat on the couch while Marlene went through the rest of the house. When she came back, he was smoking.

"Can I have a cigarette?" Marlene said.

Beckett lit one, gave it to her.

"Ben's not here, neither is Roy nor Hamilton," she said.

She sat facing Beckett. He smoked and listened to the night sounds—the whinny of a restless horse, the creaking of the house, the song of a mockingbird.

"I'm thinking about what Ben might do," he said. "He tried to hide one murder and a swindle. He only told me what he knew when we'd already found out most of it."

"You've never told me what the swindle or fraud was."

Beckett told her what Ben Scott had told him. "It doesn't seem to fit with the black market mess, and according to Dr. Remak, Captain Mark and Wicek weren't in San Vicente when Edward Radin was killed. It looks like separate problems joining."

"Ben is certain Roy did the swindle?" Marlene said.

"He says Roy was the only one who could have done it," Beckett said. "Something sent Roy running to that hospital three weeks ago. It couldn't have been the black market people, they weren't after Roy then. The black market, even new facts, couldn't have been what sent him off the deep end again."

"No," Marlene said. She seemed to shiver. "Should I have seen it, Lee?" She hugged her own slim body. "I feel so alone. Ben . . . we're not man and wife now. I want to be a wife."

Beckett felt her presence, her slim body, in his back. Her eyes were almost surprised as she looked at Beckett now.

Beckett said, "What happened to change Roy about five weeks ago? How, why, did he get involved in a swindle?"

"I don't know," Marlene said, and squeezed her porcelain face between her small hands. "He hates me, Lee. Ben hates me, too. I don't want to be hated. I want—" She seemed to flow from her chair as if her body were all liquid, soft inside her dress. She was on the couch beside Beckett, her breasts against him, her lips open and up to him. "I want, Lee. Just for now. Please."

"Ben?" he said.

She kissed him, long and soft. Whispered, "I don't care."

Beckett picked her up. She was small and light.

*

Ben Scott had been driving all day. For nothing. Roy was nowhere. Ben didn't want to think what that could mean.

The ranch house was dark except for light in the living room. Ben parked and got out on shaky legs. He closed the car door, and a light came on in the dark part of the house—in the guest bedroom. The slim shadow of a woman moved across the shade. Damn her! In Ben's own house? Martin Elder? He . . .

Ben saw the movement from the corner of his eye. In the shadows of tall trees to his right. A small horse with a man on it. A shadowy man who sat on the horse in a loose, easy manner exactly the way . . .

"Roy?" Ben Scott called out. "Roy!"

The horse began to gallop away out across the dark fields."

"Roy! Roy!"

The sound of the hooves faded. Ben Scott stood and stared out into the fields. After a time he seemed to hear the hooves again. Then the sound turned into a car motor coming fast and into the ranch driveway. Hamilton's orange Lotus. Ben's second son got out of the car and came toward Ben.

"He was here," Ben said. "Roy! I just saw him. On a horse. I called. He just rode away!"

"Here?" Hamilton said, and looked out at the fields around the ranch. "It couldn't have been, Dad."

"Who rides the ranch this late? It was Roy!"

Hamilton watched the dark fields. "When I got back from Fremont, I took Janice out. Then I drove up into the mountains. I thought about how Roy knows the mountains from when he was a kid. Maybe he has a horse, is hiding out there."

Ben said, "What were you doing in Fremont?"

Hamilton told Ben about Stella Ortega. "If Roy didn't kill them, Dad, why is he hiding?"

"He has a reason, I know that!"

"Sure he does, Dad," Hamilton said. "He'll be okay, you know? Tomorrow it'll be all okay."

Ben Scott watched his son disappear around the house toward his private entrance. The rancher stood alone for a few moments looking at the house before he went in the front door.

Marlene and Lee Beckett were in the living room.

Marlene wore a red lounging robe, and her hair was loose. Beckett was near the fireplace, dressed.

"We've been waiting," Marlene said. "A lot's happened."

"I can see that," Ben said.

"See?" Marlene said. "What do you see, Ben?"

"It doesn't matter," Ben said. "Roy was outside, Marlene. On a horse. I called, but he rode away."

Beckett said, "You're sure it was Roy?"

"Yes!" Ben snapped, and then, "No, I'm not sure. It's dark. But I know it was Roy. I know how he rides. Why did he run?"

Beckett told him about Stella Ortega again, and about Dr. Emil Remak, and Captain Mark and Wicek.

Ben Scott sat down. "They want to kill him? He didn't kill anyone?"

"There's still Edward Radin," Beckett said.

"Why doesn't he surrender?" Ben Scott said. "Those men are trying to kill *him!*"

"If he murdered Radin, maybe he doesn't care," Beckett said. "Maybe he doesn't care anyway."

Ben said, "Is that all, Mr. Beckett?"

"Unless you have anything to say, to tell me."

"I don't, and you better leave now."

When Beckett left, he didn't look at Marlene Scott. The outside door closed behind him.

When Marlene Scott heard his car drive away, she lit another cigarette, watched her husband. "I won't apologize, Ben. I had a reason."

"I know that."

"No, you don't know. Beckett has ideas, Ben."

Ben Scott said, "If I didn't know you so well, I might want you, too."

"Don't you want to hear my reason, Ben?"

"No. Make your explanations to Martin Elder."

Marlene watched him leave the living room. After a time she got up and made herself a drink.

*

Lee Beckett lay awake a long time after he got home. A beautiful woman, Marlene Scott. It had been a long time since he had found a woman he wanted even once. He had wanted Marlene.

But it hadn't been him that Marlene Scott had wanted. Not him as a man. It had not been the moment of desire and need she had made it seem. A different reason.

*

Toward morning Roy Scott slipped away from where he had been watching the rooming house where Helen Sanchez and Pelé lived.

He made his way through back alleys to the edge of San Vicente, where he had hidden Stella Ortega's green Mustang. He drove over back mountain roads, and crossed the ridge into the Santa Ysolde Valley on a high fire road. The Mustang labored in the rough country.

He parked the dusty car far from any road under thick cover, and walked half a mile in the growing gray morning light to a brush-hidden concrete flood-control tunnel in the mountains. He crawled inside the tunnel to a sleeping bag among cans of cold food, and went to sleep.

17

It was noon that Sunday when Lee Beckett walked into the prosecutor's office. Tucker was at his desk. Sheriff John Hoag stood under the map of the county. They looked tired.

"I've been to everyone, and everywhere, connected to Roy," Beckett said. "Nothing. He's dropped out of existence."

"How can they all hide from the dragnet?" Hoag said, angry. "I hope to hell they haven't slipped us."

"No one gets out of the county," Tucker said.

"I don't think Captain Mark and Wicek want to," Beckett said. "Maybe we're helping them, keeping Roy bottled up."

Charles Tucker said, "Washington called me twice already. The FBI has the lid on Remak's story, but the real action is right here in our laps."

"When we get that Captain Peter Mark," Hoag said, "the lid blows off. It's big, Charley."

"Better than Ben Scott's money any day, right?" Beckett said. "On the wires and TV like D.A. Garrison down in New Orleans. You'll both be famous. The voters love famous, honest lawmen."

"We didn't make it happen here, Beckett," Hoag said.

"Well, don't start clipping headlines yet," Beckett said. "If we don't catch Captain Mark here, you'll be just a footnote. Meanwhile, I don't care if it makes *Life,* I care about Roy Scott. I don't want his death the next headline."

"What can we do to protect him if he doesn't come in for help?" Hoag said.

"We could announce what Dr. Remak told. Put it on the radio, in the newspapers. Maybe they'd all hear it, see it."

"Washington won't let us, Beckett," Hoag said.

Tucker said, "Remak's testimony proves the black market, not the murders. For the murders, the key witness is Roy Scott. They'll have to kill him anyway."

"Maybe so, Charley," Beckett said. "Well, if we're lucky we'll stop them in time, and still catch them for the cameras."

He stalked out on the two officials.

*

Captain Peter Mark lay on the floor of the farmhouse. Sergeant Anton Wicek paced at a front window. His heavy face twitched with a jumping nerve. He looked at the telephone. "How the hell much longer do we sit here?" he said.

"Until we know where to go," Peter Mark said. "Roy is obviously holed up, too, but he has to move sometime."

"Shouldn't we at least call Remak?"

"No. That Beckett knows too much about Remak and the hospital. I only just escaped after I killed Andrewski."

Wicek paced. "If we at least had a radio."

"This place is safe, has all we need—a telephone."

"Damn it, Roy could be a thousand miles away!"

"Maybe, and maybe he'll blow the whistle in the end," Captain Mark said. "Life is chance, Wicek."

"Not my life." Wicek paced. "Nice and sure."

"One manipulates chance, of course," Mark said. "You can learn tricks even from the enemy. The VC showed me the value of kids in a war."

"You sure we can trust those kids?" Wicek asked.

"They spotted Stella Ortega at the right time, didn't they? They think we're good cops, and they're hungry for our money. Kids you find shining shoes in slum bars will be reliable when you pay them more than they could make in months."

"You sure they're watching everywhere?"

"No, I'm not sure, but they're watching everywhere we know to watch. They'll spot Roy, don't worry, and then they'll call and tell us where to find him."

"I hope to hell so, and quick, too," Wicek said.

"If they don't," Captain Mark said, "we'll lose."

*

At six o'clock that evening Beckett finished driving to every stable near San Vicente and Santa Ysolde. No one remembered renting or selling a horse to a blond young man. He couldn't check out all the owners of private horses.

He finished in Santa Ysolde, and drove past the entrance to the Charro Ranch. The guests were already arriving for the party. An important party, and most of the cars that drove the dusty road toward the ranch house were big and silent.

Beckett parked for a time, but no one came out of the ranch. Only the flow of cars going in for the party.

He finally drove away toward Silver Camp Pass and San Vicente. Any reports would come into the courthouse.

*

Janice Rhine looked at herself in her long mirror. She wasn't yet over a faint surprise every time she saw the heavy curve of her hips, the fullness of her breasts in the lace brassiere. A vague shock that this was her body now.

She ran her hand across the firm swell of her belly, the way Ham liked to touch her belly and her hips, liked to hold her hips in both his hands and pull her to him. Hamilton and her future.

She raised her arms, watched the play of her muscles in the mirror. She remembered the way she and Roy had played free on open beaches and talked of their future before he had gone away, before her curves had filled, become all female.

She picked up her dress. A black party dress, short and cut low. She slipped it over her head, zipped it up the back. At her vanity table she brushed her long hair.

Her father's voice called up, "Janice? Someone to see you. I told her you're goin' out to the party."

"Who is she, Dad?"

There was a silence. "Helen Sanchez. You don't have—"

Sanchez? Janice remembered that Mr. Beckett had said . . . "Send her up, Dad. I can finish dressing."

The woman came up, appeared in the doorway. A woman in her thirties, a little heavy, but with a face that had been very pretty. A face that was closed and wary now.

Janice said, "Are you a friend of—?"

"He sent me," Helen Sanchez said. "He wants to see you."

"See me? Roy?"

"He's in San Vicente. I'll take you. He says he's got something to tell you before . . . before he goes away."

Janice put on her lipstick. Her hands shook. She looked at her face in the mirror, and down at her body in the dress. "You have a car?" she said.

"Yes."

They went down the stairs and out the front door. Jess Rhine called after his daughter, but Janice didn't answer. She got into the old blue Ford with Helen Sanchez. Helen drove fast, almost didn't see the small Mexican boy who stood out in the dirt road waving. She stopped, and the boy ran up. "You give me a ride? Where you going?"

"San Vicente," Helen said.

"Hey, damn," the boy said. "Wrong way. I'm sorry."

Helen drove on along the dirt road past the big ranch house, where the party was already crowded. Neither Helen nor Janice Rhine looked back to see the Mexican boy pull a bicycle from the field beside the road.

On his bicycle, the boy rode to the main ranch house and knocked at the kitchen door. A cook came to the door.

"Excuse, I got lost. You let me use a telephone?"

The cook nodded the boy to the telephone on the kitchen wall. The boy dialed, spoke low into the receiver: "Captain? The Janice Rhine chick goes off in a old Ford. With a Chicano dame. They say they go to San Vicente."

In the Ford, Helen Sanchez drove fast over Silver Camp Pass and came out of the mountains into San Vicente a half hour later. At the edge of the city she turned toward an area of junkyards without noticing the black Buick that came out of a side road at the bottom of the pass and followed her.

*

Charles Tucker walked his office. Beckett watched him.

"It's late, Charley," Beckett said. "Going to the party?"

"I'm damned surprised they're having the party."

"Marlene Scott knows her mind. I think you should go."

Tucker stopped walking. "You think Roy might show?"

"He's waiting for something. I can handle the office."

Tucker went home to dress. Beckett sat with the silent telephones. After a while he looked at the wall clock. It was 8:20. If nothing came in from the roadblocks or search teams in an hour, he would go to the party himself.

He heard the commotion in the outer office at 8:30. Jess Rhine pushed into the inner office past one of Tucker's staff. "Janice's gone! Run off! She was going to the party!" Rhine breathed hard, his bull neck in cords.

"Gone where, Rhine?" Beckett said.

"If I knew, would I be here?" Rhine snapped. "She just ran out of the house with some Mex woman without saying a word to me." The foreman took a breath. "I think it's about Roy Scott. Don't ask me why, I just feel it."

"What woman?"

"A Mex, Helen Sanchez. She came to the house, asked for Janice. They talked maybe three minutes, and then out they went to the woman's car and drove off fast."

Beckett was up. "Go back to the ranch. Stay there. I'll find Janice. If she comes to the ranch, call here."

"You think she has gone to Roy?" Rhine said.

"Maybe."

"Then I'll come with you."

"No you won't. You'd just be in my way."

"Damn her!" Jess Rhine said. "Does she think I worked like a dog to let her go to some crazy bastard who wants to throw it all away?"

Beckett went out.

*

Helen Sanchez was alone in the neat room of the gray rooming house when Beckett walked in.

"Where is he, Helen?"

"I don't know now," she said.

"You went and got Janice Rhine for him?"

"Yes," Helen said. She stood there in the comfortable little room, her face composed and calm.

"Once you hid him, maybe I could forget it," Beckett said. "It got Stella killed, maybe, but it might have happened anyway. But twice, no. Did you think about the danger Janice Rhine might be in?"

"I thought about it," Helen said.

"Why didn't you call me when you heard from him again?"

"I couldn't," Helen said. "He called here. He told me he had to talk to Janice Rhine. A last favor, he said. He wanted to see Janice Rhine once more, he said. Then he'd be out of all our hair, no more trouble. He said if I didn't get her he'd be dead by dark. If I told anyone, and they came to where he was, they'_ f___d him dead. What would you have done, Mr. Beckett?"

Beckett said nothing. What would he have done? What did the law say she should have done? Follow the law, report the fugitive, never mind any consequences?

"He sounded bad, sort of bitter and hopeless," she said, "and he sounded like he meant it. I thought about the girl, and I thought about getting Pelé and trying to take Roy ourselves for his own good. But that was maybe riskier than going with the girl. I know he thinks a lot of Miss Rhine. I don't think he'd hurt her."

"Not him, damn it," Beckett said. "The others!"

"Others?" Helen said.

"The two who killed Stella are after him, Helen. What chance does he have against those two? What chance does anyone they find with him have?"

"I didn't know—" She sat down. "There was a car. Out there at the junkyards where he was waiting. Roy was alone, and he took her with him in Stella's Mustang, and the other car was down the road out of sight. I saw it when it pulled out right after Roy!"

"Did he say anything about where he was going?"

"Yes, Silver Camp," Helen said.

Beckett showed surprise. "He told you that?"

"When he was driving off. He leaned out and yelled back that they'd be at Silver Camp. At the cabin."

"He *yelled* it?"

"Yes. They had to hear, those in that other car."

Beckett went to the door. "If Roy calls again, or comes here, tell us this time. No more thinking, Helen. It's too late now."

She nodded.

18

Fog was heavy in the pass as Beckett drove. Sweeping tendrils cleared and thickened, hiding the sharp curves above the deep canyons, making the lights of oncoming cars jump hazy out of the white ahead. He had to drive carefully until he started down into the inland valley and the night cleared.

When he reached the valley floor, and the fork to the right, there was no more fog, and he drove fast toward the old town of Silver Camp. He passed through the town, light and music all around on this Sunday night of week-enders, and turned into the dirt road that led to the cabin on the bank of the river where Roy Scott had met Marlene the evening that seemed weeks ago now.

The cabin was dark and silent. In the beams of his headlights he saw the green Mustang parked out in front and the black Buick on the road. He got out of his car, his pistol ready. He heard nothing. He went toward the cabin.

"Mr. Beckett?"

Janice Rhine rose up from a clump of bushes. Her voice was frightened. Beckett ran to her, pulled her down.

"Where is he?" Beckett asked urgently.

"Out there . . . somewhere."

She gestured out toward the night and the mountains, her arms bare in the party dress she still wore. Her eyes were white in the darkness, and her breasts strained the dress with her fast breathing. "He made me hide in those bushes as soon as we got here. He said they'd come here, and he'd lead them off into the mountains, and then I should run to a lighted house, and—"

"He expected them to follow—Captain Mark and Wicek? He knew they'd follow you to him, and then follow out to here?"

"I guess he did. I couldn't run, though. I saw them get out of the black car and go after Roy, and I couldn't run."

"What did he tell you in the car, Janice?"

She shook her head. "He didn't say anything to me all the way here. I don't know why he sent for me. Maybe he's really crazy. All he said was that it would be over soon, no more problems. One more act, he said. As if he talked to himself. One more little human drama. He laughed, said he was as human as anyone, after all. He said he was sorry about calling me, but I'd be okay. I asked him to go to you, get help, but he didn't even answer."

"Then he made you hide, waited at the Mustang?"

She nodded. "They drove up slow, and he sort of jumped up at the Mustang. He was right in their lights. He ran off into the trees toward the mountains. They ran after him, Mr. Beckett. They both had guns, pistols."

"Did he have a gun?"

"No, nothing. He doesn't have a coat on. I saw he had nothing in his belt, nothing in his hands."

"All right. How long ago?"

"Maybe fifteen minutes."

"That's all?" Beckett said. "You're sure?"

"He drove awfully slow, Mr. Beckett."

"Okay. Can you make it to a house? I saw one alight back—"

"I'm afraid. I feel naked on that dark road. Can I come—?"

"No," Beckett said. "Get into my car. Keep the motor running. Turn it around, and don't put on the lights. If you see anyone coming, drive off fast. You understand?"

"Yes," she said.

Beckett patted her bare shoulder. He gripped his pistol tighter, and started across the open space toward the trees. They were thick, and began to slope upward soon among the rocks of the mountains. Farther up, the trees thinned where the dry, jagged rocks took over the rough country.

Beckett was fifty yards up the first hill when the shots came from above.

A sudden fusillade of heavy firing, followed by four more sharp, quick shots.

Beckett waited, but that was all.

He climbed on upward through the thinning trees.

*

Beckett smelled the odor of gunfire at the edge of a grove of live oaks just before an open, rocky slope. There was no moon, and the slope was dark and shadowed.

He saw two men sprawled out on the slope. Beckett crawled on his belly out into the open. When he was close to the first man, he saw that the man wore an army uniform. Nothing moved in the night. Beckett stood up.

He looked down at Sergeant Anton Wicek. Blood stained the rocks around Wicek. A .45-caliber automatic lay a few feet away. Its barrel was warm, and empty cartridge cases littered the ground.

Wicek had been shot twice in the heart, the two small holes less than an inch apart. Rifle bullets. Wicek had been flung backward like a doll, dead before he ever felt the ground.

Captain Peter Mark lay ten feet farther up the slope. The slender ex-officer was on his back. Mark had been shot twice in the heart. This time the two shots were so close they could have been one shot. The captain's pistol lay in the rocks. A heavy pistol, its long barrel hot to the touch.

Fifty yards ahead in a straight line from the bodies, a giant boulder the height of a two-story building dominated the slope. Near the top there were shadowed clefts where a man could hide and see the whole hill.

Beckett walked on to the giant boulder, and looked back down the slope. Directly behind the two dead men, in the far distance, there was a gap in the hills that would have outlined them against the sky like trees on an empty horizon.

*

There was light in the cabin near the river when Beckett got back to it. His car stood in the road facing toward the main road, its motor still running. The car was empty.

Beckett walked to the cabin and went inside with his pistol before him. Janice Rhine stood a few feet inside the door.

"I saw him come back," she said as Beckett stood beside her. "I was going to drive away when I saw it was him. He came in here, so I did, too. But he won't talk to me."

Roy Scott sat in a straight chair against the back wall of the room. His blond hair was covered by a dark knitted cap. He wore a dark blue shirt and black trousers; dark sneakers, and his face was blackened with dirt. Clothes that would make him almost invisible at night. A heavy hunting rifle rested in his lap, his finger on the trigger.

"He killed them both," Beckett said. "Roy, it's all—"

Roy said, "Put the pistol on the floor."

The blond youth's voice was somber and short. A soldier taking enemy prisoners. Beckett put his pistol down. Roy inched the rifle toward Janice. He seemed surprised that she had no gun.

"They shot first," Beckett said. "They tried to kill you. You defended yourself."

Roy's mouth was crooked, as if it had a bad taste in it. "They had no chance, not against me. I lived a year in the jungle, I learned. I'm an expert killer. Mice in a barrel. Too long out of the fighting, they were soft. No chance at all. A turkey-shoot."

"They were killers, Roy," Beckett said.

"Stupid!" Roy said. "All so stupid. Empty bank accounts full of money but no life now. They hurt Stella.

She helped me. No strings, no tricks, no use for me to fill her pockets."

Roy sat as if behind a thin glass wall, alone. "Shhhhhhh, boy, it won't do any good to tell. Be real. We all want a good life, don't we? There are more important needs to think about than truth. We have to accept it, boy, live with it. To win this war for our own safety. Stop the Reds! Charge!"

He watched the bare wall as if a movie flickered there. Beckett had the sensation that he was in a dark theater watching a solitary actor on the stage deliver a playwright's tortured monologue.

Roy laughed. "A corrupt friend is better than an enemy. At least the profiteers think the right way, we know that."

He drooped in the chair like a sagging puppet. A low voice, almost inaudible. "Did I tell them over there? I'm not sure. I think I told them, but maybe I never did. Why would Mark come after me if I'd told it over there? I don't have any more to tell now than I did then. No one would listen, I had no real proof, so why did Mark come after me now?"

Beckett said, "You had no new evidence? Nothing more than you knew over in Saigon? You weren't going to tell about the black market here? You'd told it all?"

Roy cocked his head as if listening, but it wasn't to Beckett. Roy shrugged. "A crazy psycho, battle fatigue. All delusion. Just delusion, Doc Remak said. It's the way things are, let the ball bounce. Get yours. What does it matter in the end? Who's hurt as long as the money moves? Who really loses? The world loses, Doc! Can I help the whole world? No, crazy! I'll go home, take it easy, forget it."

The silent movie still seemed to flicker on the bare wall where Roy looked beyond Beckett and Janice Rhine. "We found a black market cache once. All our PX stuff, refrigerators to beer. Our guys started tossing food and candy bars to the civilian kids. A real ball to watch those kids fight for the candy. We laughed like hell.

"We had a Cong prisoner. His hands were tied, he was down squatting with two guards over him. When he saw those kids clawing for the candy, he stood up. He said something to the kids. The kids stopped fighting. They just looked at the food and candy. Our guys tossed more to egg the kids on again. The kids walked away—all of them. The Cong smiled, and spat on the shoes of a guard. The guard shot him dead.

"An ARVIN interpreter told me what the Cong had said to those kids—'Don't crawl, don't take their leavings and their bribes. Have pride, spit on their food. Be hungry in your own country. Your country and mine, not theirs. Do not touch their candy.' He had pride, that Cong. He was a better man, but he'd have killed those same kids with a smile if they had fought against what he wanted."

Roy looked at Beckett, and then at Janice Rhine. His face all at once in the present, in the room with them.

"At the university," he said, "they told me that Ben was wrong. Marlene was wrong. Their values and actions were bad. But Ben was my father, I loved him, believed him. Who was right in the end? The difference was there in what they said about Vietnam—was it right or wrong? So I decided to go and see for myself. I saw. The lies, the hate, the horror, the greed. I told. Or did I? Was any of it real?"

He waited for an answer. If there was one, it was in his own mind. "The Doc made me better. Go home, Roy, and live your own life. Eat, sleep, work, walk on the beach, forget what no one can change. Go home where it's peaceful and no one has to kill. No one has to kill at home —but they do! Use everyone. All a big, hungry pocket to put everyone else in!" His haunted eyes begging for an answer, getting none.

"What made you go to the hospital, Roy?" Beckett said.

Roy's mouth moved like something stiff and wired. "I couldn't tell! No! I just . . . I had to get away . . . go . . . but—"

The cords in his neck were thick with effort, like a man trying to force himself through a barrier. "They didn't let me go. No, not them! So . . . I had to find Doc Remak, tell him he was wrong—there was no home where no one killed. All the same. All Captain Marks! Everyone, and—"

He shook his head violently, "What did Mark and Wicek want? Why did they hurt Stella and Ted?"

Beckett said, "They thought you had new proof against the black market operation. You told Andrewski you had a mistake to fix, fences to mend, and that people would listen to you this time. Dr. Remak thought you were talking about the black market in Vietnam, but you weren't, were you? You meant some other mistake you had to correct, had to tell about. What mistake, Roy? What were you going to tell? Was it—?"

Beckett stopped. Roy Scott's manic eyes were staring

at him like a small animal in final terror. He shrank back in his chair, crouched where he sat, his voice a thin croak. "Remak? Doc Remak? The black market over there? He was part of . . . Doc Remak? He—"

Then Roy Scott smiled.

All at once, as if a barrier had snapped, he smiled, his face bright and clear and young.

Beckett realized in the instant what had happened. Roy's mind, filled with some barrier it couldn't break, evaded by moving from life to death. His escape since the beginning, all along. Roy came to terms with the barrier by escaping the conflict, and, now, here in the cabin, he relived the moment over a month before when he had escaped the conflict by leaving the rational world as he had left it even earlier in Vietnam. Into the irrational world of suicide—the final solution to all of his questions.

For three years balanced on the line between the rational world in which he could find no answers and the irrational world where there were no questions. Slipping in and out until it became more and more automatic, a haze of reality and fantasy.

But it was not simple for Roy Scott, a boy who had always wanted to know what was inside him, and death was not enough answer. An uncertainty in him, a rock of sanity, that made him go to the hospital and Dr. Remak to see if there was some other answer. His hope for a better real world that had made him trap and kill Captain Mark and Wicek instead of himself, and that had made him plan one last act for the truth that first Monday in the Sierra before he hanged himself. But what act?

Beckett said, "Who killed Edward Radin, Roy? Not you, no. Radin tailed you to the Sierra, found you, but you didn't kill him. Someone else did, and you know who! That's why you ran—to protect the killer of Edward Radin! To make us all think you were hiding to protect yourself. Who was it, Roy?"

The youth didn't answer, didn't hear, smiled inside a remote shell. His thumb was now on the trigger of the rifle. The gun turned in his hands so that it could be aimed at his own head.

Janice Rhine cried out in the cabin, "Roy, no! Please, Roy!" She was crying.

Beckett calculated the time and distance. He would have a few seconds when Roy turned the rifle toward himself.

"Roy," Beckett said, "you called Howard Sill that night. To mend fences. Who else did you call? Who else did you have to mend a fence with before you ended it all on that rope?"

The smile faded very slowly from Roy Scott's face. His manic eyes looked at Beckett, then at Janice Rhine. Even more slowly, the rifle came down, was lowered, his thumb off the trigger. "Who else?" he said. "Who else? Only—"

The shots seemed to explode the cabin. Two shots.

Roy Scott flung forward out of the chair and lay sprawled on the cabin floor, the rifle clattering away.

The window behind Roy had shattered with the shots.

Beckett was at the window with his pistol. Janice Rhine screamed somewhere. Someone ran out in the night. A shadow stood not twenty feet away outside the broken window. A shape. Beckett fired.

The shadow, shape, cried out, seemed to fall, then was up and away among the dark trees.

Beckett ran out of the cabin. He ran toward the trees. A car started along the dirt road toward the highway. A powerful car. It ground gears, roared away, and was gone. Beckett ran back to the cabin. There was blood on the ground. He went into the cabin. Janice Rhine held Roy Scott's hand. The youth was unconscious. Beckett kneeled down to examine him.

"His pulse isn't bad," he said, explored the two wounds: one in the shoulder, one low in the back. "The shoulder isn't bad, neither is the bleeding. It all depends on that back wound. He's strong. Are you okay, Janice?"

She nodded.

Beckett began to rip up Roy's shirt. "The phone works, Janice, you call an ambulance, a doctor and the sheriff. Find a blanket if you can."

Janice made the calls. She came back with a blanket. Beckett held pressure on the wounds with wads of Roy's shirt to stop the bleeding. They covered the unconscious body.

"The one who shot?" Janice said.

"I hit him," Beckett said, stood up. "Now I'll go and get him. You stay here, and when Roy's in the ambulance, you bring the sheriff to the Charro Ranch."

19

At the Charro Ranch roasts turned on barbecue spits, and a ten-piece band played for dancing beside the pool. Most of the guests were middle-aged or older, and they neither ate nor danced. The people who moved the nation, they talked to each other and kept the six bartenders busy.

People who go to important parties feel that the importance of the party derives from the fact that they themselves are there, so no one can say where anyone else really is at any given time. No one cared where anyone else was. To be seen, not to see, was what counted.

So when the single shot echoed above the music, those who even heard it looked only at themselves to be sure that no one had shot them.

For a brief moment the party quieted.

But there were no more shots, and each important

guest saw that he had not been shot, and the party quickly gathered its strength again, and went on.

*

Beckett parked among all the cars massed along the driveway and the dirt road. The party rocked in full cry on the patio. Beckett went into the house. He walked through the rooms and found no one. At the far end of a long hallway he saw a small knot of people gathered around an open door. He walked to the group, pushed through them in silence, looked into the room.

Hamilton Scott lay on a bed with blood on his ruffled dress shirt, and blood thicker on the right leg of his dinner suit. A small man with a doctor's black bag was cutting the trouser leg. Ben Scott stood over the bed, his soft round face pale. Marlene Scott sat on the bed, touching her son. Hamilton grinned up at her through tight teeth. Martin Elder stood apart in a corner, his handsome face blank and neutral. Jess Rhine was near the door, keeping the curious knot of guests out of the room.

Beckett saw the broken window on the far side of the bedroom. Glass on the floor under the window showed that it had been broken from outside. There was blood on the rug on the side of the bed away from the window. The doctor began to fill a hypodermic syringe.

Beckett went out and around the house to the broken window. The flowers under it had been trampled. There was blood on the flowers. A thin trail of blood led toward the mass of parked cars. Beckett went back inside, walked through the curious guests, pushed past Jess Rhine without speaking, and walked up to the bed.

"What happened?" he asked.

"Lee!" Marlene Scott said. "Someone shot Hamilton! We heard the shot, and Hamilton was right here in this room!"

Hamilton Scott smiled wryly. "Looks like I was the target for tonight, Mr. Beckett."

"Damn it, go and catch whoever it was!" Ben Scott swore.

Beckett said, "Tell me the details, Ham."

Hamilton shrugged, winced. "I was bored at the party, Janice still hasn't shown up, so I came in here to be alone. I was standing near the bed when I heard a noise outside. The window broke, and—boom! I was shot. I fell behind the bed. I guess that saved me. I was covered by the bed. All I saw was a face at the window—dark, with dark eyes and hair."

"Like a Mexican?"

"Maybe, yes."

"Pelé Nascimento or Helen Sanchez?"

"It could have been one of them," Hamilton said.

Marlene Scott said, "Could it have been . . . Roy?"

"No," Beckett said. "Why would someone shoot you, Ham?"

"I don't know, Mr. Beckett. Maybe it was just a prowler, a thief because of the party and all, the jewels."

"No more talking now," the doctor said, testing Hamilton's leg to be sure the local anesthetic had taken effect. "I'm going to get the bullet out here."

They were all silent in the room as the doctor worked smoothly and quickly on Hamilton's wound. Ben Scott and Martin Elder looked away. Jess Rhine at the door flinched, his bull neck flushed. Many of the curious guests left the doorway. Only Beckett and Marlene Scott watched it all.

The doctor dropped the bullet into a basin, began to dress the wound, talked. "A few weeks you'll be fine, Hamilton. No bones or arteries hit. You can stay in a hospital a day or so, then rest here."

Beckett picked up the basin, looked at the bullet. It was a pistol bullet in good shape. He put it in his pocket. "No," he said, "he can rest somewhere else. That bullet's from my pistol. I shot him."

Hamilton looked at him. "Everyone heard the shot, Mr. Beckett. It was someone at the window there."

Beckett's voice was tired. "You fired your own rifle, yelled. A lousy trick, but all you could try. A gunshot wound is hard to hide. You couldn't just disappear for a while."

Everyone in the room was watching Beckett now.

Marlene Scott frowned up at him. "Are you serious, Lee? No, it's ridiculous!"

Ben Scott said, "What are you talking about, Beckett?"

"Hamilton faked the shooting here. I shot him out at the cabin in Silver Camp," Beckett said. "He organized that land swindle in your office, and he just shot Roy at the cabin."

Now they all looked at Hamilton Scott.

"Roy?" Ben Scott said. "Shot? Is he—?"

"He's alive at the moment," Beckett said. "Why, Ham?"

Hamilton said, "I've been here at the ranch all night. Ask Marlene and Ben. Ask anyone!"

"Of course he's been here, I saw him!" Marlene said.

"No," Ben Scott said slowly. "He was here before eight o'clock, but I didn't see him later. I thought he was off somewhere with Janice Rhine. I looked for him." The businessman-rancher was staring at his younger son.

"You didn't know Janice wasn't here either?" Beckett said.

"No," Ben Scott said.

Beckett looked at Jess Rhine near the door. "Mr. Rhine?"

"Ben didn't know. Marlene and Hamilton did," Rhine said.

Beckett nodded. "Hamilton followed Jess Rhine to me, and then followed me to that cabin. It's the only way he could have found Roy. When Rhine told him Janice was gone, he guessed that the only reason Janice would run off like that was Roy."

"No, I was waiting for Janice," Hamilton said.

Beckett said, "I was getting the picture anyway. Captain Mark and Wicek didn't kill Edward Radin. They had nothing to do with Radin. He found Roy on his own, working on the land fraud, and followed Roy to the Sierra Motel. Radin learned the truth about the swindle there, or was about to, and that's why he was killed."

He turned to stare down at Hamilton on the bed. "You were looking too hard for Roy, working too hard to convince me that Roy was insane. You were the only one who kept insisting that Roy had always been unstable. You wanted us all to believe that Roy was really crazy, that he hanged dead men!

"When you found me in that house in Fremont, you

said Roy had called to tell you where I was. Roy wouldn't have done that. He wanted me out of the way then. No, there wasn't any phone call from Roy. You had followed me to Fremont, Ham. You probably followed Roy away, but must have lost him. You came back to that house in Fremont to try to find some lead to where Roy might have gone. The telephone call was an excuse for me because you knew I was tied up in the house, and for Marlene to explain where you were going. You only brought her with you because you didn't have a good reason not to. She wanted to come with you, and it would have looked suspicious if you'd refused to bring her.

"If we check, we'll find that when Marlene called Sheriff Hoag to tell him I'd caught Roy at Silver Camp, you were in Hoag's office, staying close to Hoag. You heard that I was bringing Roy into San Vicente, and you went out to the pass and tried to kill Roy then by shooting at my car. Tonight you tried to kill Roy again. All along you've wanted Roy dead so that he couldn't tell about you."

Hamilton lay on the bed with his bandaged leg out in front of him. He started to speak, and stopped. He laughed.

"Tell what, Beckett?" Ben Scott said. "What could Roy tell about Hamilton?"

Beckett lighted a cigarette, smoked. "At that hospital, Roy decided to commit suicide, end it. But he wanted to 'correct a mistake' first, mend some fences, leave the world with the truth he valued so much, make people see the way they really were. Dr. Remak thought Roy meant the black market in Vietnam, but Remak was wrong. The land swindle here was what Roy was going to 'correct.' Roy knew about it, had been part of it in a way, and before he killed himself he was going to tell the whole story."

Hamilton Scott laughed again. A meaningless laugh. A sound, a noise, something to break the moment.

"I've got my bullet," Beckett said. "Janice Rhine saw me shoot at the cabin. There's blood out there, Ham's blood, it can be proved. We'll find the rifle Ham used on my car, and to fake the shooting here tonight. We'll find the money he made on the swindle. Sooner or later we'll find Ham's partner in the swindle. Roy is still alive, he'll talk now."

Ben Scott said, "Ham?"

"God damn it!" Hamilton Scott said.

*

Hamilton Scott's voice was annoyed, angry at his rotten luck. Something wasn't fair, no. He seemed to be trying to understand what was so unfair under the shock in his boyish eyes.

"I knew this guy Walt Ujcic around the tracks where I raced the Lotus. Walter Payson he called himself, too. He had some land in the county, and we got to talking. He wanted to sell his land, wondered if Ben would buy it. I said maybe if it had oil on it, like the land Ben already had. Walt said if he had reports like Ben's land had, he could sell it to anyone. That's when we got the idea."

Hamilton moved restlessly on the bed as no one spoke, as if trying still to understand what had gone wrong. "It was a great idea! We both saw it right away. Fake up Walt's lousy land with real mineral reports from Ben's files, and sell it to Scott Management! Ben had so

200

much land he'd never even notice a few phony parcels. And we figured why stop there? Walt said the county was full of greedy suckers. We could buy up more land, fake the real mineral reports with extra parcel numbers, and sell them. Even if the marks did scream, and Walt said they wouldn't, he'd be long gone, and what could they prove against me?"

He seemed to wait for applause. None came. He looked petulant. "Anyway, I couldn't get the reports myself, but Roy could. Only I wasn't so sure he'd take to the idea, so I told him I wanted the reports to study up and show Ben I could do the work. He was glad to help me, the big brother! Walt Ujcic made the copies, doctored the originals. He knew his work, boy!"

Beckett said, "Why do it two ways? Copy and doctor?"

"Well," Hamilton explained, "for the outside suckers we had to show them originals to make them sure they were getting an under-the-table steal, but we didn't have to attach copies to the deeds. To sell Scott Management we had to attach copies. They were supposed to be originals, but I gave Roy a song-and-dance about the originals being lost. He bought that like everything else I told him. Why not, I'd figured he'd trust me, you know?"

"Your brother, yes," Ben Scott said, his voice like some empty desert now. "How did you get Roy to okay the deal?"

Hamilton grinned, pleased with his scheme, as if he'd forgotten what had happened. "I told him I knew the phony company, that I was getting a commission on the sale! I told him I'd checked out the land myself. Then

Walt did all the business by phone and mail. With me vouching for Walt, Roy swallowed it—long enough, anyway. When he spotted the tampering on the originals, guessed we'd swindled Ben, too, it was too late. Walt was gone, I had the money, and if Roy squealed, I'd say he'd been in on it all the way. It was sure to look that way. I had him. He had to keep quiet, and it was all smooth."

"Smooth?" Ben Scott said. "A stupid trick like that?"

Hamilton glared at his stepfather from the bed. "Sure, you'd say it was stupid because it was my idea! All mine!"

Ben Scott's dry voice said, "Why, Ham? Why?"

Hamilton waved his hands. "Money in the bank! *My* money, *my* idea! You never let me run anything. You never gave me real money when you're loaded! We're rich, and I had to beg for the lousy bucks even for my Lotus. It's all for me, isn't it? I was tired of waiting for my share."

Ben Scott walked away into a corner. Marlene's eyes followed him, a kind of accusation in them. No one else seemed to have anything to say, listening and watching with bright, curious eyes. Martin Elder was watching Marlene now.

Beckett said, "All right, what happened about Roy?"

For the first time Hamilton looked uneasy. He moved on the bed, shifted, as if he were held by ropes, tied down by his wounded leg. Then his whole muscular body sagged.

"I had him, no problem," he said, "only he started acting funny, you know? Moody, not working, and then that arson trick with Andrewski. I got scared. If he cracked, he could tell. I hoped they'd send him somewhere for the arson, but Mother and Ben got Hoag to let him off free! Then . . . then I found out Ben had spotted the fraud. I knew I was in trouble, damn it. So I told Roy to remember he'd go down with me. He just stared at me, crazy-like. It was weird, I tell you, and then he just vanished! Gone."

Hamilton watched the wall in front of him as if reliving the moment Roy vanished. "That was great, you know? I mean, it was fine. Ben was sure to think Roy had pulled the whole deal on his own, and then had run! Clover. Sure . . . until that Ed Radin showed up. I knew then that Ben was going to dig until he found Roy and the whole story. I was finished. I'd be out of everything if Ben found what I'd done. Maybe even jail. No way I could even get to Roy!"

Beckett said, "Until Roy came back to the Sierra on Monday."

Hamilton bit his lips so hard, there was faint blood. A noise at the door of the bedroom made them all look. Sheriff Hoag and Janice Rhine stood in the doorway. She looked at Beckett with a thin smile to say that Roy was alive. Hoag looked at Beckett with a question. Beckett shook his head, turned back to Hamilton.

"You learned that Roy was back," Beckett said.

Hamilton said, "He was back. He was crazy. He killed Radin. You were all after him. If you caught him he'd talk. I'd lose it all, go to jail. I had to find him first."

"To kill him like Edward Radin?" Beckett said.

"Radin?" Hamilton blinked. "Roy killed Radin, you were after him, a crazy murderer. Why let him tell, ruin me? All I had to do was kill him. He was dead anyway. Kill him and I'm safe, the only son, *all* mine! I was with Hoag when Mother called from Silver Camp. I had my rifle in my car. I went to the pass, shot at your car. But Roy got away again! I looked and looked and couldn't find him. Then Jess Rhine told us about Janice running off tonight. I knew it had to be to meet Roy. I followed Jess, then I followed you. I watched you all in the cabin. I saw Roy start to shoot himself. You stopped him! I had the rifle, I tried to shoot him, but I couldn't! I couldn't shoot!"

His boyish face was a mask of fear and misery. "I shot in the pass, but . . . it was different. I shot at a *car* in the pass. Tonight it was Roy sitting there, and I couldn't shoot!"

He was crying. The tears poured down his face from fear and from anger; for the weakness that hadn't been able to shoot to protect himself, and for the strength somewhere inside that, in the end, would not let him kill his brother to protect himself; for his brother, and for himself.

"Roy didn't call you on Monday night?" Beckett said.

Hamilton's head shook back and forth—no . . . no!

"Roy called Howard Sill at four A.M.," Beckett said, "and he called someone else. Radin and Remak had followed him, but no one else knew he was at the Sierra unless he told them. He made another call to mend a fence before he hanged himself."

Beckett looked at them all. No one spoke. Beckett said, "On Wednesday, sick of running and hiding, he called two people. To talk, hear their voices: Marlene and Janice. It has to be one of them he called on Monday night. Janice, he called you."

The girl stood like a statue. "No, he didn't—"

"He called you, and you went to the Sierra. He's alive, Janice. He'll tell it all now. He—"

Jess Rhine moved from the wall where he stood. "Roy called Janice, Beckett, yes. But she didn't go to the Sierra. I did."

20

The foreman stood in the room with his weathered face impassive, his neck rigid in his rough work shirt.

Beckett nodded. "Yes, you're the only one besides Hamilton with a motive to kill Radin, and the strength to do it the way it happened. You followed me to that cabin tonight, just as Hamilton did. Before you shot Roy, I saw by his face that he *had* called someone else on Monday night, and I saw that it had to have been Janice. But she couldn't have lifted Radin to hang him, so it had to be you."

No one spoke in the room. Jess Rhine wasn't the stuff of cheap thrills. Sheriff Hoag only watched the foreman.

"It was past four A.M. on Monday," Jess Rhine said. "Who called my house past four A.M.? So I listened on the extension. It was Roy. He was crazy, saying he was going to finish it all, but first he had to fix a mistake, go clean. He was sorry for Janice and Ham, for having to hurt Ham, but in the end it would be best even for Ham."

Janice Rhine moved toward her father. "I was afraid if I told about Roy's call it would hurt Ham somehow. So I—"

Jess Rhine looked at his daughter, his tough face stern. She stopped moving.

"You just keep quiet, girl," Rhine said, looked back at Beckett. "I'd heard something about trouble in Ben's office, and Roy said he was going to hurt Ham. Janice and Ham mean a lot to me. So I went to the Sierra. It takes half an hour from here even driving fast on empty roads, it was almost five A.M. when I got there. The blond guy, Radin, I found out later, was there with Roy. I snuck up to a window, heard what I never wanted to hear."

"That Ham had planned the swindle, had used Roy, and that Roy had run away so he wouldn't have to tell what Ham had done," Beckett said. "Roy told Radin that?"

"Yeh," Jess Rhine said. "All wild, talking like a nut, the rope hanging there from the beam, and Roy wearing nothin' except his shorts! Roy told Radin that he had a letter he was leaving for Ben, telling it all. Radin tried to talk him out of the suicide, but Roy pulled a gun out of his suitcase, told Radin to get out, to go and try to save his own life! I guess Radin scared easy, because he came out of there fast."

Rhine's powerful, leathery hands opened and closed, the knotted muscles in his forearm standing out. "All my life I worked for other guys. My kid had a chance to have the Charro. Ham was her man. A crazy bastard who turned his back on all I wanted was going to ruin Ham!

Let him kill himself, good riddance—but there was that letter to Ben Scott, there was Radin who knew, and I had to think fast. I figured I could scare Radin silent, let Roy hang himself, and grab the letter! With Roy a suicide, Ben'd have to believe Roy pulled the swindle!"

The foreman's fists clenched. "So when Radin ran out, I hit him. The fool tried to fight. I hit him again, hard, twice more, slammed him against the wall. Roy heard the noise. He came out with that gun. I had to dive behind Radin's car. Roy saw me, but I guess he didn't recognize me. He—"

"He thought you were someone else," Beckett said.

Jess Rhine said, "He went back inside. Maybe he was going to do it, hang himself. Then I heard a window open. I went and looked in—Roy was gone! He wasn't going to kill himself. I ran around to the rear, down to the beach. Then I heard a car start back at the motel. He'd doubled around, taken Radin's car, was gone. I found the letter in the cabin, he'd left it. When I came back out, I saw Radin was still down. I checked him—he was dead!"

The foreman's eyes were like empty sockets. "His head hit the wall, a rock in the garden, something. I had the letter, but Roy was on the loose, and Radin was dead! What the hell could I do? I saw the rope still hanging there. Roy was out of his skull. No one knew I'd been there, they'd think Roy killed Radin! So I carried Radin inside and strung him up—a real psycho trick. I hid Radin's clothes to make it look like Roy wanted people to think Radin was him. Then I went home.

"Maybe Roy'd still kill himself, and I'd be clear. Maybe the cops'd kill him. Maybe I could still get him myself. Only I couldn't—he stayed out of sight. Then I saw it didn't matter, no one knew I'd been there, not even Roy. I was safe."

"It all pointed to Hamilton," Beckett said. "You'd done it to save Hamilton, but that didn't matter any more, did it?"

"To hell with Ham, it was my skin now! I was safe! Only tonight that woman came for Janice. I knew she was from Roy, and if Roy and Janice talked, they could figure out it was me killed Radin. So I went to you to see if you could find Janice. I tailed you, and shot Roy in that cabin."

Jess Rhine looked at Ben Scott, Marlene, all of them. "I didn't mean to kill that Radin, I didn't want to kill Roy. You found out about Ham's stupid swindle. I guess it was all for nothing. It got started, now it's finished. I hope Roy's gonna be okay."

Janice and Sheriff Hoag both went to the foreman. Janice got there first, put her arms around her father. Hoag waited.

*

Beckett, Tucker, and Sheriff Hoag were in Tucker's office. Jess Rhine and Hamilton Scott were in the county jail. The morning sun was bright and warm.

"I won't go for first degree on Jess Rhine," Tucker said. "Ben Scott's making good on Ham's swindle, no charges. We've got a bulletin out on that Walter Ujcic, or Payson. Ham's got to be a little sick, but he'll stand trial on the shooting in the pass."

"I think we should play it all quiet," Sheriff Hoag said. "Ham and Roy are both a little crazy."

"Scott family dirty linen," Beckett said. "No need to broadcast that, eh? No headlines. You both work in the county."

"It's a county matter," Hoag said blandly, unblinking.

Tucker said, "Roy had no real evidence against the black market operation after all?"

"No more than he'd had in Saigon. He never had any ideas about bringing it up again,'" Beckett said. "Remak just jumped to the wrong conclusion and panicked, whistled up Captain Mark and Wicek. They were all too scared. That's the trouble with scheming and running scared, you see danger where it isn't."

Tucker swore, "Damn, why the hell did Roy run and hide when Radin was killed? Why'd he run instead of killing himself?"

"He ran because he was irrational, confused, acting in reflex to danger, escaping," Beckett said. "He hid at first because he thought it was Hamilton he saw kill Radin. It was all Hamilton at first—he hated all Ham had done, but he couldn't turn Ham in for murder. It took him two weeks to decide to get out of it by suicide, and turn Ham in for the swindle, and then he thought Ham had murdered Radin, and he couldn't tell that about his brother. Then Captain Mark and Sergeant Wicek got into it, killed Ted Andrewski and Stella Ortega, and after that Roy hid only to get them."

Hoag said, "Self-defense. They were trying to kill Roy."

"Self-defense?" Beckett said. "Hell, Roy stalked those two like a pair of rabbits. He spotted them using those kids to watch for him. He sent Helen Sanchez to Janice because he knew they were watching Janice, knew that they would follow Janice. She was bait, Hoag, nothing else. He sent for her just as bait for Mark and Wicek to follow. He made sure they knew he was going to the cabin at Silver Camp, and he let them see him at the cabin—unarmed. Then he lured them into the hills where he had his rifle hidden. He shot them down like pigeons, no chance. It was all a trap, but they did shoot first, so maybe you can make it work as self-defense."

Hoag said, "It doesn't matter too much. Roy'll go to a mental hospital anyway—for a while at least."

Tucker said, "There wasn't any real connection between the two parts of the case, was there? Just accident."

"No," Beckett said. "It was all one package, Charley. Hamilton pulled his scheme, and that sent Roy off the deep end and back to Dr. Remak. It made Roy feel suicidal, made him decide to 'save' Hamilton by telling all he knew about the swindle. That made Dr. Remak jump to his wrong conclusion about Roy telling about the black market operation, and bring Captain Mark and Wicek around. A chain, Charley, once Hamilton got it started."

Hoag said, "What the devil made Hamilton do it? What made Roy react so crazy?"

"Maybe Roy can tell us," Beckett said.

*

Roy Scott lay in the bed in the Intensive Care Unit. He was out of danger, but he was far from recovery. When they had told him the whole story, Roy had said nothing.

Now, as Beckett, Hoag, and Tucker came in, Roy lay with his dull eyes fixed up toward the ceiling of the room. Janice Rhine sat on the bed near him. Marlene Scott stood far off in a corner. Ben Scott hovered between her and the bed.

"How is Hamilton, John?" Ben Scott said to Hoag.

"Scared," Hoag said. "He wants your lawyers. Tucker'll work with them. Ham needs help, just like Roy."

"Yes," Ben Scott said. "Thank you, John."

Tucker said, "What made Hamilton try that swindle, Mr. Scott?"

"Made him?" Ben Scott said. "Greed, what else? Beckett heard him—stupid greed, the idiotic need to be a big man!"

They all heard the strange sound. Roy Scott lay in the hospital bed looking at them. The blond youth was laughing. His drawn face etched with pain, and laughing.

"What made Ham do it?" Roy said. "The way it is did. You did. You! You made him to see nothing wrong if he could get away with it! He was proud of himself, he was going to get away with it, beat everyone. Now you'll go out and fix it, get him off. What you can get away with for the Scotts."

He lay back, breathed slow and hard.

Beckett said, "Was that what happened to you, Roy? You couldn't tell about the swindle, but you couldn't live with it, either, so you went on that arson with Ted Andrewski, hoping to get caught, be punished? You wanted to be punished, sent away, but your mother and Ben got you off? They cheated the law, fixed the world for their own needs?"

Roy studied the ceiling of the room. "They fixed it! Ben and Marlene. Ted went to a mental hospital, I went home. They cheated for their own advantage. How could I blame Ham? How could I blame Captain Mark? How could *they* blame anyone doing anything, condemn anyone? The cheating, privilege, and power that got me off made Ham what he is. The immorality. Take care of your own, get for yourself!"

He turned his face to the wall. Ben Scott watched him. Marlene Scott took a cigarette from her handbag, lit it, and walked from the room. Hoag and Tucker followed her out.

"You killed Captain Mark and Wicek," Beckett said.

"Maybe I'm no better than anyone," Roy Scott said to the wall. "They killed Stella. They hurt her."

"Roy?" Ben Scott said. "It's not all bad. Not all."

Roy didn't turn. "I went to Vietnam to see what was true in this world. I saw—privilege, corruption, self-interest and death. But Dr. Remak treated me, and he made me think I was wrong, it was all an aberration over there, a mistake, an isolated evil."

Roy turned now to look at Ben Scott. "I always believed you were a good man. I saw that the world you back is wrong, but maybe you really do want to change it when you can. I came home with that, but you don't want to change it, you and Marlene. Over there wasn't an aberration, it's the same here. You say you want freedom, but you run a repressive, destructive world. You want freedom for *you!* You say you believe in people, but you act only for yourself! Maybe it has to be that way, maybe that's the way people are. If it is, I don't want it! The lucky people never get born."

Beckett said, "If you don't get born, you're not lucky or unlucky. You're nothing. You can do nothing."

"There's nothing to do!"

Ben Scott looked at the floor. Beckett shrugged.

"Roy?" Janice Rhine said. "That poem you sent me.

Last night, after my Dad told what he'd done, I read some more of what Kenneth Patchen wrote. I read another poem of his:

> I believe in the truth.
> I believe that every good thought I have,
> All men shall have.
> I believe that what is best in me,
> Shall be found in every man.
> I believe that only the beautiful
> Shall survive on the earth.

The poem seemed to float in the hospital room. Roy Scott lay rigid. Then he moved his hand, a gesture of hopelessness.

"Roy?" Janice said. "What's best in you *can* be in every man. If there's one, there can be more. If you live, maybe you can help make it happen. That's a reason to live."

Roy said nothing. After a time his hand reached out and took Janice's hand. Ben Scott went to a window.

Beckett left the room.

*

Marlene Scott stood up the corridor with Martin Elder. As Beckett walked up, Elder stepped back, silent.

"Well," Marlene said to Beckett, "it's all over. Hamilton is in jail, Roy hates me—and Ben? I suppose Ben and I have been over for a long time."

"I wouldn't know," Beckett said.

"After the other night? It isn't Ben I want, is it?"

"You don't want anything except what you want,"

☐ Mike Gannon Series #1
BLOOD FOR BREAKFAST
Dean Ballenger

Forget about the wealthy and influential people: Gannon isn't interested in them, they can take care of themselves. He protects, defends and fights for the little guy — and girl . . . .

(#95276 — 95¢)

☐ **LOVE ME AND DIE**
Day Keene

She was a girl on the make in the city of make-believe-Hollywood. A fast-paced novel that contains everything: Murder, sex and mayhem.

(#95287 — 95¢)

☐ **TOUGH COP**
John Roeburt

They never had it so good — the crooks, the grafters, all of New York's underworld: Johnny Devereaux was retiring from the police force after 21 years. Devereaux was a tough cop. rough to encounter — impossible to bluff.

(#95281 — 95¢)

☐ **SAINT ERRANT**
Leslie Charteris

Simon Templar, handsome, debonair and very exciting, is back again as The Saint. This time he helps a maiden in distress and finds himself trapped between the police and a lady as dangerous as she is lovely.

(#95268 — 95¢)

ABOUT THE AUTHOR

JOHN CROWE is a former magazine reporter who worked most of his career in the East. When he turned to novels about contemporary America, he moved his family to a small California city. Wanting a quiet place to work, he found, instead, his subject matter. Choosing novels of suspense because he believes that people and society can be "seen and known" by their violences and their needs, by how they react to their troubles and problems, both personal and public, Crowe wanted a "place" to write about. He soon realized that in joining the flow to California he had found his place—"Buena Costa County."

The very surge of growth, change and turbulence that is California today has made it the "typical" America. All that is happening in the country happens in the small, old-yet-new cities and counties of California—faster, with greater intensity, more clearly and openly. Half-rural and half-urban, historical yet transient, in the shadow of Los Angeles, but removed, too, from that modern metropolis, the old and the new, the past and the future, the local and the alien, the aged and the young confront each day in California, and, in the suspense novels of John Crowe—in "Buena Costa County."

"Good and hot. This place is for Chicanos."

"Chili should be hot," Beckett said.

Helen brought a bowl of chili. "Is it all over, Mr. Beckett? Roy's okay?"

"He's alive," Beckett said. "I need a beer."

Helen brought him a beer.

"There's still you, Pelé, and Howard Sill," Beckett said. "You all helped a fugitive. I think I'll let Sill alone."

"And us?" Helen said. She wiped the counter.

"You're addicts. You knew the risk."

"We knew."

"I checked your clinic," Beckett said. "It's got a chance, but it needs help. I guess you need some help, too. Maybe there is a difference between justice and law sometimes. Anyway, it's worth a try to see if you make it."

Helen said nothing, but she nodded. Beckett finished his chili and beer, stood up. "Stay clean, Helen, don't break any more laws. A man like me can only lean so far."

He paid, and left the diner. It was a poor, dirty place to work, but Helen Sanchez didn't seem to think so.

Beckett said. "The other night was nice, but what did it have to do with me? When I told you about the swindle, you knew it wasn't like Roy, but you realized it could have been Ham. You took me to bed to stop me asking more questions. But it was nice."

"All right." Her eyes were brittle. "What does that make me? A tramp, or a mother protecting her son?"

"It makes you what you are—a woman who uses men as steps on a road to what she wants. Upward. But you'll never be satisfied, you're too restless. You'll always want more."

Her smile was as brittle as her eyes, or her careful blond hair. "After I've done all I can for Ham and Roy, which probably won't be much, look me up in New York. Drop in on Martin and me sometime. We'll have a party."

"A good one, I expect. You two match each other."

"Do we?" she said.

She turned to Martin Elder. The handsome executive gave Beckett a bold glance over her shoulder. The two of them went on down the corridor toward the exit, elegant and confident.

Ben Scott came from the I.C.U. room. The small rancher watched his wife and Elder disappear through the exit door. He didn't seem too disturbed.

"Have I got a chance, Beckett?" Ben Scott said. "With Roy? With Hamilton? A different life?"

"I don't know," Beckett said.

"I've wanted to change for a long time now, really live on the ranch. A romantic throwback to the frontier past, I suppose. Maybe it was *my* father who made the mistake. The ranch, and my sons."

"The sons will take some time," Beckett said. "Hamilton'll have to get some sentence, you never know what it'll do to him, how he'll react. He could go good, or go bad."

"By himself this time," Ben Scott said. "I can wait."

"Roy's a long way from stable. He could decide to kill himself again any time. Janice reached him in there, but it doesn't have to mean anything."

"I can try," Ben Scott said. "That's something."

Janice Rhine walked up to them. Her face was no longer boyish. A woman's face, tired and drawn, but turned only to the future now.

"How is he?" Beckett asked.

"He's fine now," she said. "He's really the strong one, you know, Mr. Beckett? He's Roy, he always will be, with his truth and his purpose, you know?"

"You'll stay with him now, Janice?" Ben Scott said.

"With Roy?" she said. "No, Mr. Scott, I'll stay with Hamilton. I can help Ham, and I guess I do love him. Roy's right, you know, with us it was just kid stuff. Roy doesn't need anyone to help. Do you think I can see Hamilton now, Mr. Beckett? And my father?"

"Go to Tucker," Beckett said.

She said, "What'll happen to Hamilton?"

"Who knows?" Beckett said. "That's up to him, and you."

*

Helen Sanchez was behind the counter of the greasy-smelling diner when Beckett sat down on a stool.

"You going to eat here, Mr. Beckett?" she said.

"If the chili's good."